I0543229

THE COLLECTOR OF TEARS

Stories by
Michael C. Keith

Underground Voices
2014

Published by Underground Voices

ISBN: 978-0-9830456-7-0

Printed in the United States of America.

Author's Note

Stories in this volume first appeared in *Crisis Chronicles, Blue Hour Anthology, Fiction on the Web, Smokebox Magazine, Primal Urge, The Literary Yard, Running Out of Ink, Mystic Nebula, Boston Literary Magazine, Fear of Monkeys, The Penmen Review, Lowestoft Chronicle, CC&D Magazine, Short Humour, McStorytellers, Farrago Magazine, Open Road Review, Infinite Press, Connotation Press,* and *Yareah Magazine.*

A grand tip of the hat to my remarkable readers: Nicki Sahlin, Christopher Sterling, and Susanne Riette. They get it right when I get it wrong, so they've been very busy people.

Also by Michael C. Keith

Everything is Epic
Sad Boy
Of Night and Light
Hoag's Object
And Through the Trembling Air
Life is Falling Sideways
Norman Corwin's 'One World Flight' (with Mary Ann Watson)
The Radio Station
Sounds of Change (with Christopher Sterling)
Radio Cultures
The Quieted Voice (with Robert Hilliard)
The Next Better Place
Dirty Discourse (with Robert Hilliard)
The Broadcast Century (with Robert Hilliard)
Queer Airwaves (with Phylis Johnson)
Talking Radio
Waves of Rancor (with Robert Hilliard)
Voices in the Purple Haze
The Hidden Screen (with Robert Hilliard)
Signals in the Air
Radio Programming
Global Broadcasting Systems (with Robert Hilliard)
Radio Production
Broadcast Voice Performance

And all my endeavors are unlucky explorers
come back, abandoning the expedition;
the specimens, the lilies of ambition
still spring in their climate, still unpicked;
but time, time is all I lacked
to find them, as the great collectors before me.
— Keith Douglas

Contents

THE COLLECTOR OF TEARS

Old Men Gnawing on Crullers

As the great eye of heaven shined bright,
And made a sunshine in the shady place;
Did never mortal eye behold such heavenly grace.

— Edmund Spenser

For several years, Burt, Fred, and Chuck had rendezvoused each morning at the Center Street Dunkin Donuts. The retirees referred to themselves as the Stale Donut Club, and only Fred had missed more than a few days of the early morning soirees, and that was due to treatment for prostate cancer. All three seniors considered their daily get-togethers an essential part of their twilight years, though none would readily admit that it was the high point of their day. All were single; two were widowers after long marriages.

"'Bout time you got here, you old crow," spouted Burt to Chuck, who was seldom at the donut shop at the designated time—7 AM.

"Had to take the Rockette back home," replied Chuck, with a mischievous wink.

"Oh, she came by to empty your bedpan, huh?"

The men chuckled and continued with their spirited dialog as the clock reached 8 AM. At the moment they ordered another round of refills, a Lambert Trash Removal truck was emptying barrels at the top of Summit Street. The steep residential lane came to an abrupt end directly across from the Dunkin Donuts. On two occasions, cars had plowed into the building having lost their brakes upon descending the steep hill. Fortunately, no one had been seriously injured, some cuts and bruises was all. However, a series of concrete abutments were in the process of being constructed along the sidewalk in front of the fast food restaurant.

*

The elder buddies stopped talking while the young waitress filled their cups with steaming coffee. Then their discussion resumed with its usual animated, if cynical, tone.

"It's a nasty world," grumbled Burt, picking up on their conversation about the recent spate of homicides in their neighborhood.

"You sound like a bitter old fogey," taunted Chuck.

"He's right though. Look what's out there," said Fred, pointing out the window to the busy urban street. "Boarded up stores. Litter all over the place. And this used to be a decent borough. Whole damn world is going to hell."

"Another bitter old fart," chided Chuck.

"Does make me bitter. I mean there's not much positive going on out there. Nothing to feel great about."

"Yeah, all that foolish talk about a just world. Where, I'd like to ask you? All you hear about is murder and mayhem."

"Like that book says, 'Bad stuff happens to good people. Fate is fickle,'" observed Burt.

"All those self-righteous Bible wavers talking about a compassionate God and miracles. Hogwash! There are no miracles, no mysteries. Just ugly reality."

"All the sugary donuts you guys eat and you're still bitter," observed Chuck, shaking his head in mock disgust.

"Oh, you're such a Mary Poppins. An old goody-two-shoes."

"Take off those rose-colored glasses, Chucky," cajoled Fred. "It's a cruel world, my ancient friend."

***

The garbage truck began its descent on Summit Street moving toward the next trash containers. When the driver applied his brakes, nothing happened.

"Oh, mercy!" blurted the middle-age man behind the wheel, as he frantically pumped the unresponsive brake peddle.

The truck began to pick up speed and the panicked driver looked around in desperation as the truck plunged toward Kyle Street. The old friends in the donut shop took no notice of the garbage truck speeding in their direction.

"You got that right, Fred," added Burt, emptying his cup. "Just a soulless universe."

Within a few yards of the intersection, the garbage truck ground to a sudden inexplicable stop. By that time the driver had long since leapt from his runaway vehicle. The truck sat there, engine running, but not moving.

The old men left their table and headed for the door, totally oblivious of the near disaster.

"Maybe you guys are right. It does seem like nothing really extraordinary ever happens in the world anymore," said Chuck, bidding his fellow Stale Donut Club members goodbye for the day.

"*Shit* happens, Chuck. That's what *happens*," grumbled Fred, turning and walking away.

Across the street, the driver of the garbage truck finally caught up to his fugitive vehicle.

#

Colonel Hiram's Companions

And to a remoter time Bequeath,
like a sunset to the skies.
— Percy Bysshe Shelley

The Spanish moss hanging from the sprawling Southern Oaks nearly concealed the sweeping veranda of the Colonel Hiram House in St. Landry Parish. The elderly plantation owner cut at it with a sword he had acquired from the dead body of a Union soldier a few years earlier during the Civil War. Exasperated that he was being deprived the view of the eastern expanse of his homestead, he chopped at the ubiquitous growth with a force that belied his age.

"Let me do that for you, sir," offered his servant, Thomas.

"I'm still capable of using this Yankee blade," replied the Colonel, swinging away.

"Yes, sir, I knows that, but it gonna make you ache cause of your rheumatism."

"Guess you're right, Thomas. About got it all, though. Maybe just cut a little more there to your left."

"Yes sir, I do that right now."

"Thank you, Thomas. I do appreciate your concern for my wellbeing."

For ten years, the Colonel had resided without family or loved ones on the Hiram plantation. Alone except for his two former slaves, who chose to remain in his service due to a lack of any other options, the seventy-five-year-old had sunk into a deep melancholy over his isolation. The absence of close company had weighed so heavily on him that he longed for his passing and had even considered bringing it about before it arrived on its own.

He continued to dearly miss his wife, now gone a decade, and to mourn the fact that they never had children. *What a comfort they would be now to this old man*, he lamented, loading his pipe and lighting it. *We just couldn't make any youngins, could we, Belle? Though we never stopped trying, even after we knew we were barren. The Hiram name will die with me … and so be it. Sooner the better, too.* What other relatives the Colonel had were either dead or had long ago moved away from the Parish to some unknown locations in Louisiana and even further. He had few friends left now because of his intensely close business and personal relationship with his wife. Besides, he'd lost touch with them years before.

Hiram spent most of his time reminiscing about his days in the Confederate Army and as a grower of cotton and sugar cane. After his Belle died, he lost interest in growing crops to sell. His wife had been the driving force behind the operation, managing the books and overseeing the needs of the help. Without her, he quickly found it impossible to continue with the business, so he let his fifteen pickers go and began his solitary existence. It was not long before Hiram regretted the loss of the former activity on the plantation, but he felt it was too late to return to the way things had been. He was just too old and, more to the point, at sea without his beloved partner.

*   *   *

The Colonel routinely rose just after sunrise already depressed over what he knew would be just another endless and empty day. The only human contact he would have would be with his former slaves, and he knew without their presence he would be doomed.

"Mornin,' sir," greeted Esther, as she entered the kitchen. "You ready for your breakfast? Want some honey on your grits, or just butter, Colonel?"

"Neither, Esther. Just some coffee."

"Now Colonel, you know what the doctor say. You gotta have something in your belly before you have your coffee cause of them ulcers."

"Oh, phooey. Don't like doctors. Bunch of quacks. My belly has been fine. Just got no appetite. Maybe a little later, okay?

"Yes sir, whatever you want," shrugged the middle-age woman.

She seems to be getting older, too, thought Hiram, watching her move to the stove. *Not quite the pretty one she used to be.*

"You and Thomas sure do look after me, and for that I am heartily grateful."

"It be our job, Colonel, and we fine with that."

"Don't know what I'd do without you. Glad you stayed after I freed you. Hope you don't ever abandon me. Might just as well drown me then."

"No sir, we ain't goin' no place."

"On second thought, Esther, maybe I will have some of your grits. Nobody makes them better."

"Sho' 'nough, Colonel. You be eatin' make me happy."

Your being here makes it bearable, noted Hiram, spooning up a helping of grits.

"You okay in the cabin, Esther? Seems it ain't the best place for comfort, and you and Thomas ain't getting any younger yourselves. Probably have the aches, too."

"Oh, we be fine in that old place. Been there over thirty years, so it be home to my husband and me, sir."

An unusual, if not extreme, notion had occurred to Hiram during one of his earlier darker bouts with loneliness. But he was reluctant to put forward his idea to Thomas and Esther, fearing they'd reject the proposal. *Why would they want to move in here with me? I've been their master and now I'm their employer. They are like friends, though. No, that's crazy,* considered Hiram. *Besides, think how townsfolk would react to Negroes living with me? So what? None of their damn business anyway. I need someone else in this empty house or I'm going round the bend for sure.*

Several weeks passed before Hiram gathered the courage to ask if the couple would consider moving in with him in the big house. Just as he suspected, their initial reaction was one of surprise, if not downright shock.

"I've been mighty low these last few years being alone rattling around in this empty house, and you two are as close to me as any other living beings. So it sure would be kind of you to consider moving in here with me. The two rooms in the north wing are empty and sure got to be more comfortable than that old shack of yours. I would consider it a singular act of kindness if you'd do this for me."

His former slaves were speechless for several moments, and then Esther broke the silence.

"Colonel, that be awful good of you to let us move into Hiram House, but we fine where we is."

"Wouldn't look proper if we come to live with you, sir," added Thomas.

"Nonsense. I don't care how it looks to other folks. Besides, I hardly see anybody any more, and for sure nobody ever comes out here," protested Hiram. "Tell you what, think about it for a day or two, okay? I don't make this offer lightly. This empty house is pushing me toward my grave, and having other folks, colored or otherwise, share it with me will darn sure make me feel better."

The next day Thomas informed Hiram that they would accept his offer to move in. After conferring with one another on the subject, both Esther and he felt obliged to go along with the Colonel's request. Deep down they felt they had no other alternative than to go along with their former owner's proposal. Yet as much as they liked him, they could not quite abide the idea of living under the same roof with him.

*   *   *

The years crept by, and whatever reservations the colonel's former chattel had about living with him eventually vanished. They found him to be a generous and considerate housemate, which did not surprise them. As awkward as it was at first, the three residents of the antebellum manse soon came to regard one another as individuals on equal footing. They took meals together, regaled one another with stories by the fireplace in the winters, and spent the endless summers in happy conversation and long naps on the veranda. It was a time of great contentment for all of them. Hiram was profoundly grateful that the deep loneliness he had suffered had gradually faded with the closer proximity of the Negro couple.

It was during one of those long summer days that Hiram took ill. He refused to let his companions fetch the local doctor and consequently became more infirm as days and then weeks passed. Eventually, the Colonel grew so immobile that he required Esther and Thomas to spend most of their time with him in his bedroom. He would ask that they sing their gospel songs to him, and they were pleased to oblige, yet they remained anxious because he would not let them seek medical help.

"Your sweet voices are the best cure. No doctor has that in his bag."

Then one morning when she brought him his coffee at the usual hour, Esther discovered with deep sadness that the Colonel had passed away. Honoring his request, Esther and Thomas buried the Colonel under the flowering canopy of the southern magnolia that his father had planted a half-century earlier. They had tried to convince the dying man to have a proper burial and church service, but he had firmly objected. He told them they were his only relations, and they could say a prayer for his soul's redemption at his gravesite, if they were so inclined. They were.

After laying Hiram to rest, Thomas and Esther prepared to leave the plantation, since they felt they should no longer remain there.

"We gots to tell the sheriff 'bout the Colonel before goin' down to Nawlinz," observed Thomas.

"S'pose, but he didn't say nothin' about doin' that. Could be gettin' us in trouble for burying the Colonel before tellin' nobody."

Esther and Thomas debated the issue while removing the soiled covers from the Colonel's bed. As Esther was depositing the sheets in a clothesbasket, she noticed an envelope with her husband's name on it on the floor next to the nightstand. She picked it up and showed it to him. While she could read a little, Thomas could not decipher writing at all.

"Whad it say?"

Esther closely inspected the document she pulled from the envelope.

"Oh my!" she finally blurted. "This say *we* be given the plantation. On a deed the Colonel writ his name on."

"What? How that can be?" responded Thomas, gawking in amazement at the official looking paper.

"It is, Thomas. I swear that's what it say. We be the rightful owners of Hiram Plantation now. Lord have mercy!"

Thomas and Esther sat on the veranda for several hours contemplating what to do next. Finally, Esther announced a decision.

"It our place now, so we gonna stay and live here. That be what the Colonel wanted."

"I don't know, Esty. Don't seem right."

"It right as the Bible. We stayin', sugar!"

And so they did. Several blissful weeks passed for the couple and then a stranger appeared.

"Come to call on the Colonel. Tell him Jeremy Foster Tyler is here to see him."

"He ain't here, sir," said Thomas.

"Well, where is the old fella? Can't be out chopping cane at his age."

Reluctantly, Esther revealed the truth.

"No sir, he ain't doin that. He be buried over there."

The visitor turned in the direction she pointed.

"You mean he's dead? Well, how the heck ... I mean, how come nobody knows?"

"It was the way the Colonel wanted it. Told us to bury him under that there magnolia," replied Esther, feeling her body tense up.

"That ain't right. Can't just put a person like the Colonel in the ground without a funeral. Not dignified for a person of his stature."

"We just done what he tell us, sir," said Thomas, clutching his straw hat.

"Even if he's like you say, what are you niggas still doing here? Where's his family?" inquired the man, with a bark.

"He got none, mister."

"Then you best be gettin' yourselves out of here," growled the stranger.

"No sir, we ain't leavin.' The place be ours now. The Colonel wrote it so."

"What you saying, girl? Are you just as crazy as you look?"

"Here, this be the deed, mister. All legal, and such," said Esther, placing the document before the man's eyes.

"Well, we'll see about that. This don't sound right. You niggas up to something, huh?"

The man tore the document from her hand and trudged back to his horse.

"We'll see what the sheriff says. If you know what's good for you, you'll get your black asses out of here in a hurry."

Thomas and Esther watched as the man galloped out of sight.

"We better do as the man say, muttered Thomas."

"The devil we are! This be *our* place. The Colonel give it to us legal. They'll see what writ down in the deed. Right is right!" countered Esther, returning to the kitchen.

A full night and day passed and they began to feel somewhat better about things since no one had shown up to challenge their continued existence at the plantation.

"It be okay, honey," said Esther reassuringly, as they turned in for the evening.

"Well, you never can tell what them white people be up to when it comes to us black folks."

They were fast asleep when torches were thrown through several of the windows. In seconds, the mansion was consumed in flames. When the sun rose, there remained nothing of the stately structure but a pile of burning embers. Esther and Thomas's bodies were never found, and it was assumed that they either managed to escape somehow or they were burned to ashes.

Decades later, the unclaimed estate was purchased by Noel Culpepper—the patriarch of one of St. Landry Parish's wealthiest families. The plantation remained undisturbed for several years until the new owners built a lavish home just a few feet to the east of where the former Hiram House stood. But on the very day the wealthy Culpeppers were to move in, their new house mysteriously burned to the ground.

"Bet it was Hiram's goddamn nigga ghosts did it," declared Noel Culpepper, recalling the legend that had circulated since Esther and Thomas had vanished nearly a half-century ago.

Out of the smoldering remains of the newly constructed mansion appeared another structure that no living being could see. On its veranda sat three diaphanous figures smiling warmly at one another. After a moment, the old friends turned in the direction of the unobstructed view that lay before them, and their smiles grew.

#

Dying Day

Eternity was in that moment.
— William Congreve

TAKE THE DREAD OUT OF DEAD! TAKE THE CRYING OUT OF DYING! SCHEDULE YOUR PRACTICE DYING DAY NOW BY CALLING 1-800-DEAD-DAY. DON'T WAIT UNTIL IT'S TOO LATE, read the huge digital billboard along Route 95 between Boston and Providence.

That catches the eye, thought Clayton Gray with satisfaction. The twenty-nine-year-old Rhode Island native recorded a reminder into his 9G iPhone ("Order more signs.") while maintaining a speed a good 20 mph above the posted limit.

His franchise of Dying Day Centers was growing rapidly. Three years ago he had come across an article in the *Wall Street Journal* that set him on a completely new career path. He had worked at a small law firm up to that time but had been eager to get in on something that might substantially increase his income. Now he owned four DDCs in southeastern New England and had plans to open more.

Before Clayton had finished reading the *Journal* article, he was convinced the concept was brilliant. It was something everyone wanted … *needed. Who wasn't afraid of dying?* He immediately went on DDC's website, where the home page repeated his exact sentiments and offered a solution to the universal conundrum:

Afraid of Dying? Most everyone is, but you don't have to be. A simple one-day Reorientation session will put you at ease as you face life's end. You can remove the horror of the final moments before departing this world and entering the next …

23

The website continued to enumerate the benefits in eliminating the anxiety associated with dying, promising to make it a fear-free, even pleasant, experience:

> *Be at peace as the end approaches. Enjoy the final moments with your dearest thoughts instead of being gripped by terror and apprehension. DDCs guarantee a happy ending. Call now to set up your pre-Dying Day interviews. It will change how you view your own demise ...*

Clayton had excitedly clicked the "Business Opportunities" link and soon found himself contacting the franchise office's 800 number. Two months later, he opened his first location in Warwick, Rhode Island, and three months after that a second in Barrington. The next two followed quickly. The money started pouring in and plans were in hand to expand into surrounding states.

It's like the movie Soylent Green, recalled Clayton after he had made first contact with the company. Loving science fiction, it had been one of his favorite films, and the scene in which Edward G. Robinson lays atop his deathbed as his most desired experience is fulfilled, had always stuck with him. *What a way to go. Dying while your best thoughts are played out.* He had been excited to think that soon he would be a part of a business that offered such a humane service.

*   *   *

The road was nearly empty at 3 AM Sunday morning as he returned from his Casual Connect date. It had turned into much more than a cappuccino at the mutually agreed upon bistro on Charles Street. A night of unharnessed lust left him exhausted but content. He pulled off the highway to find a Dunkin' Donuts for a large blast of caffeine. It didn't take long to find one. They seemed to have stores at one-mile intervals. Clayton hoped his Dying

Day offices would one day be as ubiquitous. He chuckled at the realization that both businesses shared the same initials.

"No one can be finer, 'cause my Dinah is a minor, Deedee Dinah," sang Clayton as he arrived at the drive-up window and placed his order. As he sipped his hot coffee back on the highway, he belted out a variation of the tune. "Nothing could be finer than to be in her vagina in the morning." *How good can life get?* he pondered as the Providence skyline came into view. *Home for a quick shower and then on to the Warwick center.* It was Clayton's practice to participate in as many reorientation sessions at his various facilities as possible, although he had very capable staff members at each location. He took great pride and pleasure in being an active part of the exceptional service. Relieving clients of their greatest fear made Clayton feel like he was making a great contribution to the human race.

"Can there be any greater profession?" chirped Clayton pulling into his driveway. "No, absolutely not!"

An hour later he reached his DDC headquarters in Warwick and was greeted by Carla Harcourt, the receptionist and his personal assistant. She informed him that his first REO (the abbreviation had been inspired by Carla's favorite rock group—REO Speedwagon) was waiting for him in the Pre-REO suite. After dropping some things off in his office, he greeted the elderly client, who had invested the required $2500 for the procedure.

"Mr. Jenkins. You've had your DD interviews and now are ready for your Reorientation. Is that correct?" asked Clayton, warmly.

"Oh, yes. I'm more than ready."

The two Dying Day interviews involved a lengthy series of questions to determine a client's greatest fears and joys—in the first instance, something to be avoided, and in the second, something to be fully realized. After compiling a comprehensive profile of the individual, the Center would prepare a digitized virtual experience of what was most precious to the client. During the actual REO session the client would be placed in a sensory deprivation chamber where he or she would remain until acclimated to the absence of stimuli. The DDC termed it Death Simulation. It was intended to create the impression that one was removed from the living world. The oxygen in the chamber would be decreased in prescribed increments to simulate the collapse of the body's ability to breathe and replenish itself. The client's heartbeat would be monitored to insure there would be no actual cessation of life. At the peak of the client's anxiety, the specially created video containing the client's notion of profound happiness would be rolled. Oxygen would then be fully restored as the client was immersed in his beatific vision. When the client reached what was termed a Bliss Line—as reflected by a very relaxed pulse rate—the video would slowly fade away. A soft, reassuring voice would then repeat—in mantra like fashion—"There was never anything to fear." REO seldom ran over an hour.

When the chamber door was opened, the client was often found weeping with joy and appreciation. Repeat sessions were available to those who desired them, but for most a single REO was enough to sustain an individual through the balance of his or her life. The service had not been in existence long enough to see if this would actually be the case, but so far only one client had requested a second REO. In the end, he cancelled the session without giving a reason.

*   *   *

Following the day's first REO session, Clayton had lunch and met with a new client, who looked very familiar to him. Halfway into the first interview, Clayton realized who it was. When he was eight years old, his third grade teacher, Mr. Houser, had fondled him on two occasions in the cloakroom. Clayton had been too confused and frightened to tell his parents, and then he was saved from further molestations when his parents had switched him to the local Catholic school. Now he sat face-to-face with the pedophile and his heart began to race. He abruptly ended the first meeting, saying that he didn't feel well. It was either that, or go postal on the man, figured Clayton.

Carla scheduled the client's second meeting for the next day, while Clayton sat in his office contemplating the encounter. He had always thought about the two shameful incidents with Mr. Houser, but never took any action on the matter, even though he figured his former teacher was still in the area. The more he thought about the childhood incident, the more he wanted to retaliate. Then it came to him. He would give Mr. Houser an REO session he would never forget.

When his long-ago teacher appeared for his second meeting, Clayton gathered all the information he felt he would need to execute his revenge.

"So, Mr. Houser, what are the things you fear most in life?" inquired Clayton.

After a long pause, the teacher answered. "Spiders and snakes really freak me out. Even the tiny harmless ones make me feel like fainting."

Well, we share that in common, thought Clayton.

"What else, Mr. Houser. Try to be specific."

"Well, let me think. I really don't fear much. Maybe getting caught … ah, for something I really didn't do."

"Like what?"

"Oh, you know. Being accused of something bad and being put in jail."

"What might that something *bad* be, Mr. Houser?"

The gray haired man shifted in his seat, and then waved Clayton off. "Nothing … really. Who knows? Can we get on to the next question, please?"

"What other things frighten you?"

"Like I said, I really don't get scared by much … except by spiders and snakes," said Houser, appearing agitated.

"Okay, let's shift gears to something much more positive. What gives you the most joy in your life?"

"Children. I used to teach grade school. Retired now."

"Children? How did they give you joy?"

"They're so sweet and innocent … really beautiful. Just looking at them would raise my spirits. I adored them."

"All right then, what else contributes most to your happiness, Mr. Houser?

"Fifi."

"Fifi?"

"My Shih Tzu. She's the real love of my life. I've never been married, so my pets mean everything to me. I've had four dogs and loved each one dearly."

"Anything else makes you real happy?"

After several seconds of contemplation, Mr. Houser replied. "Can't really think of anything else. I mean, that gives me as much pleasure as children and Fifi."

Following several more routine questions, Clayton said he would schedule Mr. Houser's REO at 8 PM the next day.

"Oh, you do the sessions in the evening?"

"Only occasionally," replied Clayton, "but our schedule is so full at the moment, we're forced to do so."

"Wonderful. I'll be here then."

When Clara asked about scheduling Mr. Houser for his REO, Clayton said the man had decided against having one. Despite what he had told his former teacher, REOs were never scheduled after 5 PM. However, for this customer, Clayton was more than happy to make an exception, and he needed to be alone to initiate his plan.

*   *   *

When the center closed for the day, Clayton went to work in the digital mixing suite. His goal was to prepare a video hologram for Mr. Houser's REO session that would be like none he'd ever made before. If Clayton's plan succeeded, it would increase Mr. Houser's fear of dying tenfold—and Clayton's satisfaction at least as much. He worked long into the night gathering images that would horrify Mr. Houser while in the sensory deprivation chamber. They included the most ferocious pictures of spiders and snakes he could find, including several action images of large snakes devouring small dogs. He had even come across a gruesome video of an Anaconda gulping down a Shih Tzu.

After a couple of hours of sleep in his office, Clayton continued to refine his hologram for the man who had marred his childhood. Fortunately, his day's schedule was open, except for one client interview, so he had more than enough time to prepare the special REO. By late afternoon, Clayton had completed a video that he felt would haunt his third grade teacher to his grave.

At the designated hour, Mr. Houser appeared at the Dying Day Center for his REO session.

"So this will really make a difference in my life? I've always had nightmares about dying, and if I don't any longer, it's going to be wonderful," said Houser.

"Yes, it will certainly change how you see your death. I can assure you of that," said Clayton, leading his client to the REO chamber.

Mr. Houser entered the small cubicle with noticeable hesitancy.

"I'm not fond of small spaces."

"Nothing to worry about. I'll be monitoring you just outside."

After Mr. Houser took up his position on the padded catafalque, Clayton attached a series of wires to his temples and chest and then departed the chamber.

"Just relax, Mr. Houser. This will be an unforgettable experience for you. You'll never think of death in the same way."

Clayton took up his position at the REO control panel and viewed Mr. Houser through a window and also on monitors connected to an infrared camera in the chamber.

"Happy dying, you fucking pervert," muttered Clayton, leaning back in his chair.

He allowed for a longer than usual period of "void" time to have it's effect and then activated the hologram. By that point he had reduced the oxygen level in the chamber by thirty percent, causing Mr. Houser to gasp for air. Within moments his erstwhile nemesis was screaming at the horrific images that enveloped him. Clayton averted his eyes from the scene. It had been all he could take to assemble the footage of snakes and spiders, and he could no longer tolerate the sight of them. He thought it ironic that he and his molester shared the same dark aversions.

Sounds of horror and desperation poured from the REO production room speakers for the next hour. By the time Clayton finally entered the chamber, Mr. Houser had fallen silent.

"Mr. Houser. Your session is over. You have been reoriented."

When Clayton reached his subject, he believed he had fainted from the horrific sights he'd been subjected to. *Maybe he's dead*, thought Clayton in a sudden panic. But then Mr. Houser spoke.

"That was good ... *really* good. It has changed my thinking about death just as you promised."

Clayton was perplexed by Mr. Houser's response.

"Good?"

"Yes, just what I needed. Now let's give you something you need."

His former teacher stood and looked at him across the short expanse of darkness. His eyes cast an eerie glow, causing Clayton to take a step backward. In that instant, Houser lunged at him striking Clayton's forehead against the wall. The force of it made Clayton fall onto the cushioned recliner. As he did so, he felt the hands of his attacker groping his genitals. Before he could react, he received another powerful blow to his head, which rendered him unconscious. As he sunk into a nightmare state, he heard a hideous, otherworldly cackle.

"It's time for your Dying Day session, my little third grader," growled Mr. Houser, leaving the chamber and locking its door.

Before he fled the control room, he pressed the activate switch on the equipment console and saw the chamber come alive with the grisly images that had been assembled for his exclusive benefit.

*   *   *

When Carla returned to work after the long weekend, she discovered her boss's self-mutilated cold body lying in the REO chamber. On the video monitors was a grainy photograph of Clayton as a happy eight-year-old.

#

The Collector of Tears

Put my tears in thy bottle.
— Prayer Book

While Googling the subject "rituals for the dead," undertaker Miles Chartley learned that gathering the tears of mourners was an ancient tradition predating Christ. Intrigued, he saw fit to revive it as an additional service of his business. *The dearly departed will spend eternity with the essence of your love*—read the Chartley Funeral Home brochure. If mourners consented, and they usually did, their tears were collected in a glass vial as they flowed from their eyes. The tear bottle was then ceremoniously placed with the deceased before the casket was sealed.

However, the precious liquid never left the building, because Miles had other plans. Before a coffin was put in the hearse for the trip to the cemetery, he would remove the vial and place it in a locked refrigerator he regarded as his *lachrymatory*. After discovering the existence of tear bottles, Miles had engaged in further research on the subject. It resulted in his coming across an obscure Norse myth that held that tears of sorrow possessed rejuvenating power when imbibed.

It had been many years since Miles began drinking the yield of mourners' lacrimal glands, and he was certain it had slowed his aging. Confirming his belief was the solicited judgment of those who worked for him that he did not look fifty-eight years old.

"You must have a portrait of yourself in your attic," came the frequent response to his calculated inquiry.

Something better, mused the never-married mortician. *Something much better.*

When business at the funeral home inexplicably slowed down—*people stopped dying because of the bad economy*, Miles quipped to his underlings—client interest in the preservation of their tears declined proportionately. The latter concerned Miles more than the former. The legend proclaiming the restorative value of lamentation fluid had made it clear that the procedure had to be done at least once a month to have the desired result.

When the parents of a deceased hemophiliac had the corpse brought to his funeral home, Miles was relieved. They had heard about the tear bottles and insisted one be placed in their daughter's coffin. The weeping at the service was so prolific Miles could easily have filled several bottles, but one was all that was prescribed by the ancient sources he had consulted. He carefully adhered to the tenets of the myth fearing that violating them might compromise the outcome he keenly desired.

∗ ∗ ∗

After the service, Miles removed the vial from the deceased woman's coffin and stored it away for later use. His mood was greatly improved as he led the procession to the cemetery. That very morning he noticed the lines around his eyes and mouth had deepened, and their reappearance had caused him despair. He was excited that the remedy to his problem now awaited him upon his return.

As soon as he dismissed his two member staff, he went to the refrigerator for the mourners' tears. He removed the vial and was stunned to see that its contents had turned crimson. "This can't be!" he cried out, rechecking the cooler's empty interior. *It must be contaminated ... cursed*, he thought, carrying the bottle to the small pond in back of the funeral home. There he sat on a bench and stared at the ampoule. *No good. It's no good. I can't drink this stuff*, he lamented.

For several minutes Miles pondered his predicament and then uncorked the container, pouring its contents into the man-made pond. A cloud blocked the sun as he stood looking into the murky water. "What!" he blurted as the pond began to turn the color of the liquid he had emptied into it. Within seconds it looked like a huge cauldron of hemoglobin.

Miles thought he noticed something move in the pond, and he stepped back in apprehension. Soon the carcasses of several small fish and frogs surfaced. *How can this be?* he wondered, and then his eyes caught sight of a moving object at the other end of the pond. He strained to see what it was, and what he saw made him question his eyesight. A naked woman slowly climbed from the scarlet water and faced him. For several moments neither moved.

Oh my God, it's her! Anna Kowalski, The girl I just buried, concluded Miles, his entire body trembling.

The woman stared at Miles and her beauty was balm to his jangled nerves. He tried to grasp the absurdity of the situation, but what was occurring was far beyond his comprehension. *This can't be. It just can't be*, he told himself, beholding the resurrected corpse just a few yards away.

"What are you? How can you be alive?" he managed to utter.

The response came in the form of an anguished moan that tugged at his heart.

"Don't move. I'm coming to you," said Miles.

He walked toward her through the high grass lining the pond's edge. The closer he came to her the more he was taken with her loveliness. Never having been in the presence of a live naked woman, he was amazed at how different she looked compared to all the female cadavers he had worked on, and it excited him. When he reached her, she looked at him with a mixture of confusion and need.

"It's okay," assured Miles, trying to avert his eyes from her supple breasts. "Let's get you inside."

He removed his jacket and put it over the woman's bare shoulders. He then led her to the back door of the funeral home and up the stairs to his private quarters on the second floor. All the while, Miles felt like he was in a dream world. *Is this real?* he kept asking himself. The young woman remained silent, except for a soft whimper.

"You'll be okay. Sit here on the couch and rest," said Miles, placing a quilt around her lithe body.

It can't be the dead woman. It just looks like her, Miles tried to reason.

"I'll make some hot tea. Just sit there. I'll be right back."

When Miles reentered his living room, he found the mysterious woman asleep, the quilt fallen off her lower extremities. Her posterior was as perfect as anything he had seen in magazines or movies, and he sat across from her and took in a sight so magnificent to him he swelled with excitement.

What should I do? fretted Miles. *She has relatives and friends. What about them? Maybe I should contact them and let them see her. Would they believe she's here and alive? Maybe they wouldn't know this woman.*

Miles remained seated across from the slumbering specter attempting to come to terms with the bizarre circumstances in which he found himself. It took all of his will power to resist the urge to touch her flawless and perfectly shaped derriere. When she began to awaken, he got up and returned to the kitchen. There he made noise to create the impression he had not been gaping at her nakedness while she slept. After a couple of minutes, he reentered the living room and found her sitting on the couch with the quilt around her ankles.

"Uh ... do you feel better? Is there anyone you want me to call? Your name is Anna ... Anna Kowalski."

Miles's questions went unanswered, and he was at a loss as to what to do next.

"You must be cold sitting there like that. I mean I keep my apartment cool. Don't like a lot of heat. But that's me. Maybe you'd like to wrap the quilt around you. It's there on the floor," he said.

Anna remained impassive.

Call the police, Miles. She might be psycho.

"Can I get you anything? You can call someone to come and get you," offered Miles, lifting a cordless phone from the coffee table.

It was then that he discerned a change in her languid expression. Her eyes focused on him and her lips parted slightly in what was almost a smile.

"Yes, that's right, talk to your family, Anna," said Miles, moving the phone closer to her, but she made no attempt to take it from him. "They would want to hear from you, although I think they may be shocked you're ..."

She shook her head almost imperceptibly.

"No? You don't want to call them?"

This time her movement was more decisive.

"Why?"

The woman's eyes suddenly closed and her body went limp. Miles went to her and checked for a pulse. *She's dead again*, he concluded with a shiver, but then her eyes fluttered open and she placed her cold hand on his. The floor beneath him seemed to rock, and he felt his knees buckle. He fell forward into the woman's breasts, and she placed her other cool hand on the back of his head as if to keep him from moving away.

The dread that had suddenly overwhelmed him just as rapidly dissipated and was replaced by a feeling of contentment. Miles moved his head slightly and took her nipple into his mouth. His sigh of satisfaction was matched by her own as her body arched to fully meet his.

I'm having foreplay with a dead person, thought Miles, and a chill rose up his spine. He pulled away only to witness his netherworld paramour fall unconscious again. *Oh, Lord*

... *Oh, Lord!* He rose and sat across from her. The woman's skin was radiant and her hair possessed a lustrous glow the likes of which he had never seen, even in television shampoo commercials.

I'll keep her. Just for while, until ... until when? Questions flooded Miles brain. *Would death finally gain the upper hand and reclaim her? What would she do next? What would he do next?*

*   *   *

SHE HAS NO PULSE! SHE HAS NO PULSE! bellowed the voice in Mile's head as he awakened in darkness. He had fallen asleep after hours of just staring at her nude body on the couch. As his eyes adjusted to the dark, he made out her silhouette. She sat erect and motionless.

"Anna?" he whispered, and she replied in a shallow voice.

"Hold me ... *please.*"

Miles rose from his chair and sat next to her. She took his hand, raised it to her lips, and kissed it. He felt an electrical charge course through his body.

"What are you? I know you're the dead girl, Anna, but ... but you're still *alive.*"

He slid his forefinger to her wrist to check for a pulse again. *Nothing! There's nothing.*

"Make love to me," said Anna, her breath cold against Miles's ear.

"I ... I shouldn't." he stuttered. "You're de ..."

Before he could finish his sentence, Anna pressed her lips against his and all resistance left him. The two were quickly entwined in a passionate embrace. For the balance of the night and throughout the following day, they engaged in lustful activity the likes of which Miles had never imagined possible. By the second day, he believed he was in love with the exquisite reanimated corpse and that fact no

37

longer disturbed him—if it ever really did. *This love is truly beyond the grave!* he joyfully mused. The surreal experience was everything he had ever hoped for and, in every conceivable way, so very much more.

"I love you, Anna!" he shouted at the top of his lungs and then his world went black.

*   *   *

After a couple of days, Marge Rubio and Paul Wilson wondered where their boss was. Miles had never taken time off or gone on vacation, so they were justifiably concerned.

"There's no answer when I knock, and I've called his number several times," explained Marge to her fellow embalming assistant.

"Me, too. He's been acting a little weirder than usual lately. Hope he's okay?" added Paul.

"He doesn't have any relatives or friends, so where could he be?"

"Maybe we should break into his apartment," suggested Paul.

"I don't know. Let's wait awhile. If he doesn't show up by noon, we'll do something."

Noon passed and Marge and Paul decided to take action. After banging on the apartment door and calling Miles's name, Paul administered several hard kicks to the lock of the upstairs apartment.

"Smells kind of odd," commented Marge, as they entered. "Turn the light on. It's so dark in here."

"Oh my God!" they both gasped at the scene before them.

Dozens of empty tear bottles cluttered the floor.

"They're tagged, too," observed Paul, lifting a couple vials for a better look. "I recognize some of the names. They were clients."

"What was he doing with them? They were put in the caskets with the bodies."

"You tell me," answered Paul.

They found more empty tear bottles in the kitchen and bathroom.

"The bedroom," directed Paul.

It took Marge a while to locate the light switch on the wall, and when she did, she wished she hadn't. Sprawled across the bed was the naked body of their employer.

"Is he ...?" hesitated Marge.

"Yeah, I think so," said Paul, moving closer to where Miles lay. "Man, he looks so old."

"Doesn't even look like him, but it is. I recognize the onyx ring on his right hand. He said his dad gave it to him when he graduated from embalming school."

"There's a stain under him," noted Paul, leaning in closer to the body. "Wish the light was better in here. Not even a window."

He took hold of Miles's shoulder and turned him over.

"Whoa! Looks like someone had a night of passion."

Deep scratches extended across his back, and blood still trickled from them.

\#

Falling from Trees

Wild animals never kill for sport. Man is the only one to whom the torture and death of his fellow-creatures is amusing in itself.

— J.A. Froude

BB guns reached their peak of popularity in the 1950s. They were nearly every boy's ultimate dream gift in the years that followed the war. It was the era of the television western, and a Daisy Golden Eagle was the foremost object of desire by legions of youngsters. Kelly Tuttle was among them. He had asked—pleaded—for one since he was seven, but it wasn't until he turned twelve that his parents finally gave in to his impassioned request.

"Happy birthday, son. Just remember, it's not a toy," said his father.

"I know. I know," replied Kelly, as he tore the wrapping paper from the air rifle.

"It can cause serious injury, so you need to be very careful how you use it."

"I will, Dad. I will … *promise.*"

"First time I see or hear of you doing something you shouldn't with it, I'll take it back," warned Mr. Tuttle, sternly.

Kelly could not wait to try out his shiny new Daisy. To him it looked exactly like the Winchesters cowboys used in the movies and on the home screen. He was delighted by its authentic appearance and imagined himself shooting menacing Indians from a galloping horse. After unwrapping several less exciting gifts, mostly clothes, he asked to be excused to go play outside.

"Of course," said his mother. "Have fun."

"Just remember what I said, Kelly," added his father.

Without a further word, he ran to his room to dress for his first outing with his cherished firearm.

$*$ $*$ $*$

"Hi Yo Silver!" shouted Kelly, holding his Daisy rifle high above his head in the middle of his backyard.

He carefully loaded BBs into the specifically marked compartment and took aim at a wide range of objects, first among them the dandelions that covered the field behind his house. He pretended they were a wild band of Apaches attacking him. After a while, he took pleasure in shooting at the new leaves that hung from the trees at the field's edge—*lions' claws*, he imagined. As he was unloading a string of BBs at a tall oak, he noticed he had struck a large blue jay. While it surprised him, it also thrilled him to have shot something alive, as he thought of it. The bird flapped about on the ground; one of its wings spread in deformity.

Finish it off so it won't suffer, thought Kelly, taking aim at the injured fowl and shooting it dead. Kelly experienced a feeling of excitement and satisfaction as he pushed the bird's corpse with his foot. He also felt pride in having shot his first wild animal. *Maybe they ate them back in the olden days.* Kelly's thoughts were interrupted by the sound of fluttering above his head. There on a limb were two more large blue jays. *They must be new ones because they're so fluffy*, he reflected, staring up at them. Suddenly the urge to kill them took hold of him. He raised his gun and fired a volley of BBs at them. Both fell dead to the ground. Elated, he inspected their carcasses. He had never felt such a surge of adrenalin, and he searched nearby trees for more potential prey. Within a few minutes, Kelly had shot three more young blue jays.

Finding no other living targets for his Daisy, he started for home proud of his successful hunt.

"You're a sharpshooter," muttered Kelly, boastfully. "You could shoot anything ... *anything*."

As he left the site of his slaughter, he was unaware that his father had witnessed him shooting the last birds. Rather than confront his son on the spot, Mr. Tuttle decided on a course of action to teach him a lesson. He scooped up three of the bird carcasses, and while remaining at a safe distance, followed Kelly home. There he waited for his son to leave his bedroom. When he did, he placed one of the bloodied birds on his bed. Later when Kelly returned to his room, he was shocked to find the dead animal. He braced himself for trouble, believing that his father had found his handiwork. When he appeared for supper, he fully expected to encounter angry parents. He was surprised and relieved when nothing at all was said about his destructive outing with his Daisy. Instead, his parents mostly spoke between themselves, only occasionally acknowledging his presence with a word or two.

After supper Kelly returned to his room and pondered how the dead bird got there. He was convinced his parents would have said something if they knew what he'd done. Satisfied that they clearly did not, he wrapped the carcass in an old shirt and slipped it out of the house, depositing it at the bottom of the trash barrel. *How did it get in my room?* he continued to ask himself, and the mystery kept him awake part of the night.

*   *   *

Nothing about the shootings was said the next day, and Kelly went to school still wondering how his dead prey had appeared out of nowhere. Despite the inexplicable placement of the dead bird, Kelly felt little remorse over his deed. But he was spooked and genuinely perplexed by what had occurred afterwards. When he reached home, his mother greeted him cheerfully, asking him if he'd like a snack. Kelly declined the offer and went to his room eager to play with his BB gun. *Better not shoot any more birds for a while*, he told himself. When he reached for his Daisy in the closet, his hand struck something unusual.

"What the heck!" he shouted, when he realized it was another dead blue jay.

What's going on? Are the birds doing this? Are they getting even for my shooting them? Kelly reflected on this as he removed the second bird's remains.

"Hate you birds! *Hate* you!" he rumbled, preparing to get rid of his feathered victim before his parents discovered what had happened.

Again, he placed the body in the trashcan, making certain to bury it out of sight. When he returned to his room, however, he found the third blue jay. *No*, he whimpered, *not again*. After finding still more dead birds in his room over the next two days, Kelly was convinced the new Daisy must be cursed. Thoroughly shaken by events, he realized to his surprise that he no longer even wanted the rifle. He returned it to his father, saying he would rather have the pair of binoculars he had long fancied.

"What do you mean you don't want it?" asked his father, slyly.

"I thought I did. But I don't like it. I'd rather have the Gundlach field glasses, Dad. Can you exchange the gun for them? I only used it once."

"I guess," frowned his father. "I still don't know why you don't want the Daisy. You wanted it so much for so long."

"I know. It's just *that* ... well, ah, I guess I'd like the binoculars more."

"Okay, I'll see if I can take it back."

"Thanks, Dad. *Thanks.*"

Kelly then excused himself and went out to the porch and sat in the rocker. Looking out over the front yard, he thought, *Someday I'll get a real gun.*

As cars drove past, he shot at them with his index finger.

Passing

His ignominy sleep with thee in the grave,
But not remember'd in thy epitaph!
— Shakespeare

Professor Emanuel Doople had taught at Marligold College his entire career—forty-seven years, to be exact. He was well liked and respected and did his best to meet his students' needs, despite his diminishing energy and declining enthusiasm for the classroom. On the morning of his final exam for his two sections of macroeconomics, he felt light-headed and slightly nauseous. He attributed it to the two glasses of Merlot he had had during dinner with a job candidate and the chair of his department the previous evening. His consumption of alcohol had always been modest and after his wife died he simply stopped drinking altogether. There was no particular reason for his abstinence other than the fact that the occasions for tipping a glass had become rare in his spouse's absence.

In recent weeks, Dr. Doople had experienced a steadily deepening sense of fatigue, prompting him to call his doctor. An appointment was set for later in the day, but he would not make it. A few minutes into his class he found it hard to catch his breath, so he went to the open window for more air. As he stood with his back to the class gulping for oxygen, he let out a resounding fart, prompting snickers and giggles from his students. When he turned around his body let out a series of equally raucous emissions transforming the class's subdued amusement into wild hysterics.

"I'm sor ... *sorry*," he stuttered, moving a couple of steps.

The elderly professor then fell forward nearly hitting a student and tumbled to the floor dead. Although he had departed the world of the living, his cadaver continued its voluble existence. Students leapt to their feet and circled their expired instructor, but no one made an attempt to revive him. On the other hand, nearly all dialed their cellphones for help. The air in the classroom had become putrid from Doople's unrelenting discharges, causing its shocked and repulsed occupants to make their way to the corridor to await the arrival of the authorities. In minutes, campus police were on the troubled scene and were quickly joined by paramedics.

"Oh man," grumbled the first rescuer to enter the classroom. "What a stench."

"He's still releasing," observed his cohort.

"No kidding. Like Mt. Vesuvius."

Even as Doople's corpse was placed on a litter and removed from the classroom, his body continued to emit toxic fumes, causing moans and chuckles from the crowd that lined the hall to the building's exit. Soon news of Doople's untimely death reached every corner of the campus, but instead of solemn observations about the longtime professor's passing, jokes were made about his malodorous departure.

On the day of his funeral the college's president, Mary Courtney, delivered the eulogy. Hundreds attended the service on the main quad and except for an occasional isolated outbreak of laughter the event was dignified. That is until Dr. Courtney said, "Students will miss Professor Doople's unique way of capturing their attention." Her words inspired a member of the audience to shout, "BY FARTING!"

Hilarity immediately swept through the assembled mourners like a tsunami, and despite Courtney's attempts to restore calm the uproar continued unabated. Soon Courtney herself was bent over with laughter as the local newspaper photographer snapped pictures of the bizarre scene. The next day the town's broadsheet carried pictures of the pandemonium, along with the headline: "Doople Funeral a Gas."

Gradually the professor's name became a popular synonym on campus for passing air—to "Dooplecate" was to fart twice or more times. A decade after Doople's demise, a statue was dedicated to his memory on the Marligold campus. At its unveiling, the president of the class of 1971– who had been in the classroom in which Doople perished– urged the small gathering to refrain from laughing. However, his speech appeared to be designed to undermine his request. With a mischievous smile, he spoke.

"Ladies and gentlemen, we are here to pay homage to one of Marligold's finest educators. As you know his legacy far exceeds his words, and this statue honoring Professor Doople will inspire generations of students to think of other prominent figures—such as Thomas Crapper and Nguyen Dung."

In 1994, the bronze effigy was removed to a warehouse to make way for a new chemistry lab. The building was not named in honor of the memorial it replaced. While recollections of Professor Doople faded, his ignominious moniker lingered like the scent of a meticulously aged Limburger.

\#

Winter is Always Coming

Ah Love! Could thou and I with Fate conspire
To grasp this sorry Scheme of Things entire.
— Edward Fitzgerald

Sixty-eight wasn't really old by 2014's standards. In fact, some people said it was the new fifty-eight. Of course, that was bullshit, thought Ed Bentley. The way he felt, sixty-eight was the new seventy-eight. His joints stiffened and ached, and he was convinced the harsh Maine weather was the major cause of his bodily woes. As he saw it, the only remedy to his failing health was a dramatic geographical change—a move south.

"I'll die if I stay up here," he'd complain to his wife. To which she would invariably respond, "And I'll die if I leave here." A tense stalemate had continued over the issue.

Both Bentleys were native Bangorites but while Edith remained content and happy with her birthplace, Ed had long ago lost his affection for the small central Maine city, largely because of his declining health. So the war of words grew more intense as Ed felt steadily worse.

"There are other places on earth, you know. This is not the only place to live, Edie."

"Well, it's the only place I want to live. Stop complaining. This is where we belong. It's our hometown."

"Let's at least spend the winters down in nice warm Florida. It would sure help with my arthritis. We could get a little condo. Real estate is cheap right now, and mortgage rates are low, too."

"But I love the winters here. You know that. And I'm the president of the Blue Hat Ice Skating Club. I'm not going to give that up."

"How about a little consideration for how *I* feel. You know I'm in pain, especially when it gets really cold," complained Ed, his frustration compounding.

"You have meds. Besides, I think it's mostly in your head, Ed. You look fine. Lord, you even did cross country last winter."

"Just that once, and I paid the price, too. Haven't fully recovered yet. Look, can't we at least go down to Florida and check out places?"

"I don't like it down there. I told you that after we went to Disney World."

"That was fifteen years ago, and we only stayed in the park. You really didn't see the state. There are some beautiful places there."

"It's beautiful here, Ed, and we don't have all those bugs. Remember those flying cockroaches?"

"Palmetto bugs. They're tropical and they don't bother people. Besides, everyone uses an exterminator and that takes care of it. You're just looking for things to complain about. Half the people we know have retired down to Florida, and they love it."

"No, not all of them. I spoke with Millie Carter the other day, and she says she can't stand the heat and humidity there and wishes they never moved away."

"Her husband loves it there. Says he feels better than he has in ages. Millie is always griping about something. She did that when they were up here. You know that, Edie. You even said so."

"I did not. Can we stop talking about this? I'm not moving south, and that's final!" said Edie, in a tone Ed knew all too well and resented.

Bitch! I don't know why I stay married to you, Ed brooded, as his wife left the room. A moment later, he went over to his good friend's house to vent. He had done so on many occasions.

*   *   *

Same old argument, right?" asked Duke Stefan, inviting his neighbor into his house.

The widowed horror writer had lived across from the Bentleys for six years, and they had become well acquainted with him. Ed had become closer to Duke because he had found he was someone he could confide in, especially regarding his issue with Edie.

"She's so goddamn hard-headed. Won't even consider my feelings. I've had it," grumbled Ed.

"You've said that before."

"Well, this time I mean it. She won't give an inch. Here I am literally dying by degrees because of the miserable winters up here, and she won't even consider spending a few lousy months away from her beloved Bangor. She just thinks about herself. Thirty-eight years of marriage and she won't compromise for my sake."

"Just leave her. Go to Florida yourself. That will end the impasse once and for all."

"I would, but …

"But what?"

"Well, to be frank about it, she has all the money … inheritances from her family. My retirement savings are pretty small."

"So, you said Florida was cheap to live."

"But we could live *really* well if only she'd agreed to move there, too."

"You can't have it all, Ed."

"But I want it all, and I deserve it after all these years with her."

"Well, there seems only one remedy to your dilemma."

"What's that?"

"Get rid of her."

"Huh?"

"Kill her."

"What? Just like they do in your novels?"

49

"There are times when it's the only way to fix an impossible situation."

"You're kidding, right?"

"Not at all. You want something from her that she's unwilling to give you, and without it you say you're going to die. So what other answer is there? It's really kind of self defense."

Ed looked out the window to his shuttered Cape and thought about all the years he had devoted to making his wife comfortable and happy. *She doesn't care how I feel. She knows I'm getting worse with this arthritis, but she won't make any effort to help me out. She's only concerned with herself, and it's never going to change, unless ...*

"How?"

"How, what?"

"How could I get rid of her? Nothing grotesque, like in your books. I don't want her to suffer."

"She doesn't have to suffer."

"Things aren't great, but we did have a lot of good, or at least, decent years together."

"Of course you did. But that's behind you, right? Now you're unhappy and she doesn't care."

"This is really crazy. I'd never get away with it."

"Are you kidding? The statistics show that the majority of homicides are never solved. It's all in the way you do it."

"For example?"

"Make it look like an accident? Maybe she falls down the stairs. Impossible to tell if she was pushed."

"I've got to go. This is crazy. I can't believe we're even talking about this," said Ed, suddenly feeling unnerved.

"So stop complaining and accept the situation, Ed."

"Hard to accept anything when you're in almost constant pain," replied Ed, displaying the swollen joints in his hands.

"Your decision, my friend. It's you or her. Winter is on its way, and it's crippling you."

*   *   *

Ed decided to make one more desperate plea to Edie in the hope that she might finally come around to the idea of spending at least some of the cold months down south, but he found her as unyielding as ever on the subject.

"Stop badgering me about moving. This is our home, my home, and I have no intention of leaving just because you have a little arthritis. Enough already! Shush!"

I'll have to do it. I'll kill her, thought Ed, his mind made up. *Push her down the stairs. Make it look like a freak accident.*

"I'm going to replace the stair runner. It's all stained and faded," said Ed, initiating his plan.

"Good idea. Do something. Get our mind off your little problems. Let me know when you get it removed. We'll go to Carpet Mart and find another runner. I'll be in my sewing room."

Ed got some tools and began removing the carpet in order to expose the hard wood steps beneath it. *If she falls down these, she won't be around to talk about it*, he thought, feeling better about his future prospects. *A little push, and Florida here I come.*

When he had removed the runner, he stood at the top of the second floor stairs and called for his wife. The second he did, however, he sensed someone behind him and suddenly he was falling. As his head slammed against the oak steps, his necked snapped. Edie stood at the top of the stairs and smiled. A moment later, the doorbell rang, and she answered it, climbing over her husband's body.

"Done," she said to the person standing before her.

"Best damn plot I ever came up with," observed Duke, embracing her.

51

For all those murdered today by unknown assailants

Fate intentionally guided
your unfortunate movements,
and you unknowingly complied
with plans designed to eliminate you.
For this day long ago had been set aside
as the day without reason
you would die.

#

Dream Lover

Thou tyrant, tyrant Jealousy,
Thou tyrant of the mind.
—— John Dryden

Lenny Boswell was awakened by his wife's restlessness. By gently nudging her side with his elbow, he was able to stop her tossing and turning. But as he was about to doze off she began talking in her sleep. What she had to say caught his immediate attention.

"Oh, Richard, I've always wanted you."

Richard? wondered Lenny. *Who the hell is Richard?*

"You're so hot looking. You've always turned me on whenever I've seen you," gurgled Ginger Boswell, slowly grinding her hips.

"What the ...?" growled Lenny, giving his wife a hard poke with his elbow, causing her to sit bolt upright.

"Huh ... what's the matter?"

Lenny was about to confront her with the obvious question but then decided not to, thinking he might get more information about the mysterious Richard if she went back to sleep.

"You were moving all around and woke me up," muttered Lenny.

"Sorry," said Ginger, lying back down and turning over.

"I can't sleep when you're jumping around like that."

"Okay, I'll ..." murmured Ginger, drifting off.

Lenny remained awake and alert, hoping his wife would offer more information about her mysterious dream paramour, but she said nothing. The next day her sleeping words echoed in his head, and he vowed to continue his vigil that night to learn more about what seemed to be his wife's secret love life.

*　　　*　　　*

Not an hour after they turned in the next night, Ginger began mentioning Richard in her sleep in terms that both riled Lenny and kept him awake throughout the night. By morning, no further information regarding Richard's identity had been revealed, and Lenny was in a foul mood. When Ginger entered the kitchen for breakfast, Lenny launched a full assault on her about her nocturnal ramblings.

"Okay, who is this Richard you're talking about in your sleep?"

"What? Who ...?" answered Ginger, baffled.

"You know, *Richard* ... the guy who gets you all hot and bothered?" snapped Lenny.

"*Wha* ... are you okay? You seem weird."

"You can stonewall me all you want, but the truth will come out. It always does," blurted Lenny, rising from the table and stomping out of the house.

When Lenny got to his barbershop, he scanned the town's White Pages for anyone with the name Richard. Since Burwell, Arkansas, had only six hundred residents, it didn't take him long to discover that there were only three Richards living in the town. He knew them all and instantly dismissed two as possible suspects. One was a paraplegic and the other was north of 90 years old. The third familiar Richard, however, managed the insurance company that held Lenny's car and life insurance policy.

Richard Sutton, he mumbled to himself. *Could be. He's about our age and not bad looking, except for the Charlie Chaplin mustache.* Lenny decided he would monitor Sutton's movements the coming Monday night when Ginger planned to get together with the girls. If possible, he might catch them in the act and have the goods on both of them. *I'll kick their god damn asses*, he growled, as his first customer of the day entered his shop.

"What's up, Len?" asked the town manager, Don Jessick.

"More than you want to know, Don," answered Lenny, adjusting the height of his barber seat.

*   *   *

During the nights that followed Ginger continued to talk about Richard in the most intimate of terms, causing Lenny's blood to boil and again denying him sleep. By the appointed Monday, he had been so deprived of rest that he felt like he was operating in a trance. The day passed slowly, and the more he anticipated exposing his wife's deception the darker his mood grew. When his last customer of the day departed, he tidied up the shop and on the way out pocketed a straight edge razor. *Someone might get a very close shave tonight*, he told himself, as he walked the block to the Sutton Insurance Agency.

Lenny took up surveillance in the doorway of an empty store front directly across from his possible rival's office. The lights were still on, and he could see Sutton sitting at his desk. He expected his wife to appear at any moment, but after more than an hour she had not. Still, he remained confident she would, that is, until Sutton's wife, Hilda, pulled up. She beeped her car horn for her husband and within a couple of minutes the Suttons had driven off, leaving Lenny more confused and frustrated than ever.

"If not Richard Sutton, then who?" grumbled Lenny, clutching his razor as he walked to his parked car. He drove the few streets of the tiny town hoping to catch sight of his wife's Toyota and when he did not see it, he drove to Silasville, ten miles to the east. It was the largest town in the county with a population twice the size of his village. He made a quick run down the main drag and then swung through the adjoining residential streets. No sign of Ginger. *What is she up to?* Lenny wondered, coming to a stop at the edge of town. After reviewing his options, he retraced his route, finally returning home just as his wife did.

"How's Richard?" he asked, as she climbed from her car.

"Who? Not that again. I was at Joyce's Amway party. Bought a few things. Here," she growled, shoving a bag into his arms.

"Didn't see your car there."

"There were a bunch of cars parked behind me, so how could you see it? Were you spying on me?"

"Nice ploy, Ginger. Did your sexy Richard buy you these things?"

"Yeah, he bought me some laundry detergent and cleaning products. For God's sake, you need to see a shrink. What's going on with you?"

"What's going on with you is the better question. All night long you're talking in your sleep about Richard. 'Oh, Richard, I want your lips on me. Oh, sweetheart, touch me. Oh, yes, Rich …'"

"Shut up! I don't know what you're talking about. I don't even know anyone named Richard," protested Ginger heading to the house.

"What about Richard Sutton? You know him."

"The insurance guy? I only met him once," replied Ginger, disappearing inside.

"Yeah, I bet," shouted Lenny after her.

*   *   *

Lenny sat alone in the parlor until he was certain his wife was asleep. He then entered their bedroom and sat in a chair next to Ginger waiting for her to begin talking in her sleep. He didn't have to wait long.

"Come to me, Richard. I need you so bad," murmured Ginger, her hands moving up and down her body. "Yes, that's it, Richard. There … right *there*."

"You cheating bitch!" growled Lenny, removing the single edge razor from his pocket and opening it.

"Oh, yes … yes, Richard! That's it. That's the spot," shrieked Ginger, ecstatically.

At that instant, Lenny pretended to slide the blade across her neck.

"My movie idol, my officer and gentleman, I will always be your pretty woman …"

"Aha, that's who it is," roared Lenny. "Richard *Gere* … you *bastard!*"

#

A Place in Reverse

Earth provides enough to satisfy man's needs,
but not everyman's greed.

— Mahatma Gandhi

In the spring the leaves and flowers in Havertown, Delaware, blossomed in various shades of gray. Indeed, all vegetation seemed to take on the color of campfire ash. Meanwhile, all man-made structures showed off in countless captivating hues—vibrant blues, opulent reds, subtle oranges, and luxurious greens. The small community north of Wilmington was a place of opposites. No one was sure why such a bizarre transformation had taken place, including the army of scientists that descended on the town. The media quickly speculated that toxins from a nearby chemical plant might have been the cause of the phenomenon. However, a team of EPA investigators had soon debunked that theory. The feds found no connection between the color reversal and what the factory had emitted into the air and surrounding soil since it began operating in the 1930s.

The citizens of Havertown tried as best they could to continue with their normal lives, but their world had been so profoundly altered by the inexplicable event that it was extremely difficult … at least at first. The biggest challenge for locals was acclimating themselves to objects that appeared in stark contrast to what they had always been—and were in most other places. Purple sidewalks lined with leaden tulips took getting used to, as did the loud primary colors of many of the town's buildings and the iridescent lime-tinted utility poles that glowed in the dark. Despite the bizarre metamorphosis, Mayor Charlie Trevor soon found an upside to the bizarre situation.

"What could possibly be *good* about this, Chuck?" asked the local florist at an emergency town meeting.

"Tourists! Since word got out about this, people are starting to flock here."

"They don't buy gray flowers, your honor."

"Maybe not, but they buy damn near everything else," declared Trevor, grinning broadly.

"There is *that*," observed Mike Temple, owner of the town's pizzeria. "Besides, I rather like my building in Kelly green. Sure can't miss it."

"All I'm saying is we should make the most of this crazy thing while it lasts. I'm sure it's only temporary. Just a fluke of nature ... or something. The people from the government say it isn't dangerous, nor toxic. The water and air are fine. Soil, too."

"So what is it, Mr. Mayor? I don't think nature behaves this way. As far as I've read, it never has in all of history," noted Havertown High School Principal Tim Jennings.

"Maybe some kind of outer space effect. Could be that we've been invaded or at least contacted by aliens," speculated a town selectman.

"Yeah, this is just too odd to explain any other way," chimed another member of the board.

"Look folks, I'm sure there's a perfectly reasonable explanation for what has happened. But all I'm saying is let's take advantage of it while it lasts. The town could sure use the revenue. We're in tight straits, as you know," repeated the mayor.

"It's always all about the money with you people," blurted Amy Clark, director of the town's senior center.

"Fine, ah ... *thank you*, Amy. Well, I think we're done here. We'll gather again when and if something further develops," said Trevor, hitting his desk with a gavel. "Meeting adjourned."

"*But ...*" stammered Clark, who then pushed her way through the exiting crowd heading for the door. "Probably the end of the world and all you people care about is making a damn buck. Well, you can't spend them where you're going."

*   *   *

News media vehicles, including those from the national television networks, clogged Havertown's main street and proved an additional attraction for curious visitors. Coverage of the town's strange phenomenon was now worldwide news, and opinions about its cause were as various as those of the town's residents. In the end, however, there was no singular theory as to why the color jump, as it soon came to be called, had taken place. Meanwhile, earnings of many of the local businesses skyrocketed to the delight of nearly everyone. The few naysayers argued that Havertown had turned into a freak show and was no longer a decent place to live and raise families.

"Our community has become a pathetic oddity for the world's curiosity seekers. It no longer is the wholesome place it once was. And chartreuse is *not* a proper color for a church. It's so inappropriate," grumbled Reverend Sylvester Howell, during an interview with Fox News.

A month after the first manifestations of the extraordinary visual mutation, the town coffers were so full plans were being made to construct a new tourist center that would house a broad range of facilities, including a restaurant, video arcade, and amphitheater. This further riled opponents of the mayor's strategy intended to exploit the situation for monetary gain.

"We should be investing in Havertown's schools. Our kids deserve better than what they have. We need computers and more teachers, for starters. The buildings themselves—no matter how bright they look—are in general disrepair and wholly inadequate," argued the head of the school board.

"That will happen. Right now we've got to fan the flames, so to speak. Visitors to our fair town will stay longer and spend more if we properly accommodate their needs," countered the mayor.

"Charlie's right," added Ben Harrison, owner of the Havertown Inn. "I'm adding a bunch more rooms, maybe twenty, and a gift shop, too. These visitors love to buy souvenirs and all that junk. We can fix up the schools when we're better set up to do the job right."

Several more merchants agreed with Harrison and the mayor, which effectively silenced their critics for the time being.

"This is good for all of us. In a few months, we'll be able to turn our attention and newfound bounty to the more basic, and yes, essential, needs of the town. We have to first optimize our income potential, and the new visitor complex will help with that," proclaimed Fowler to the large crowd assembled in the town's high school auditorium.

*   *   *

And as he'd hoped, the number of tourists did continue to grow in the months that followed. At the ribbon cutting ceremony for the visitor's center, Mayor Trevor announced another new project already known to the town's merchants, if not its general population.

"Next Spring a water park unlike any other will be built on the west side of town, courtesy of the Havertown Business Coalition. It is part of our community's continuing efforts to bring more visitors to our Eighth Wonder of the World."

The mayor had proposed the extravagant moniker, which was immediately embraced by his ever-growing inner circle of hope-to-be millionaires.

"That's what they called us on *The Colbert Report*, so I guess that's what we *are*," declared Trevor.

"Yeah, that pretty much makes it official," added Ben Harrison, who announced that he was building yet another new addition to his inn. "At this rate, I'll need a hundred new rooms."

The group of budding entrepreneurs almost squealed with satisfaction.

"And we're still in the clear because all of those nerdy scientists haven't come up with anything that says the color jump is harmful," said Curt Johnston, publisher of the *Havertown Eagle*.

"Love the color of money," whooped Howard Carlson, the owner of Howey's Ice Cream Emporium.

His statement was loudly repeated like a chant by his cronies and overheard by Amy Clark, who was passing the group's gathering place on her way home. "Damn fools!" she growled. "Should be tarred and feathered for what they're doing to this town."

*   *   *

The demands of residents that tourist profits be allocated for necessary improvements to public facilities and services finally reached a peak, and the mayor and his cronies were forced to abandon their plans to underwrite a multi-level parking garage adjacent to the visitor's center. It was during the week that ground was to be broken for the much-needed construction of a new middle school that people began to notice a subtle change in the colors that had so profoundly reversed the town's fortunes. Within a week it was all too apparent that the invaluable hues and tints on all of the buildings were fading.

"Oh my God! What can we do?" asked Harrison, panicking.

"This is the end. We're done for ... screwed," interjected Curt Johnston.

"Not for a while," said Trevor. "The media are coming back now, so things will be hopping again. *Cha-ching!*"

"Yeah, maybe for a week until we're just old news. Then what?"

"Then what, Chuck, huh?" added Harrison, sarcastically.

"We'll come up with something," answered the mayor, tentatively.

"Oh, sure. That'll be easy. We'll just paint the colors back on all the buildings and everything else. No big deal."

"Don't be ridiculous, Ben. Okay, everybody, let's all think on it. We'll meet at the end of the week right here in my office."

*   *   *

By the time the date came to regroup, Havertown no longer could boast being the Eighth Wonder of the World, as it once again looked like every other community. As its buildings faded, its foliage had regained much of its natural pigmentation. The streets were all but empty, and the media had departed sooner than expected.

"Okay, Chuck. Let's hear your big idea. How are we going to keep from going bankrupt now?" asked Harrison, as he leaned against the mayor's desk.

"Actually, Ben, it's *your* big idea," responded Trevor, with a toothy smile.

"Huh?"

"We're going to put the colors back."

"What?" exclaimed Harrison, as did everyone else in the mayor's office.

"That's right. Tonight we're going to begin painting the buildings the way they were. And we're going to spray the trees and plants with herbicides.

"That's insane," balked Mike Temple.

"Holy crap! You think that will fool anybody?" blurted Johnston.

"It's either that or we're all going Chapter Eleven. How are you guys going to maintain your expanded businesses when there are no tourists? Huh?"

"But, jeez …"

"*Jeez*, nothing! We have no alternative. Without the influx of tourist dollars, we're done for. Now here's the plan. I ordered all the paint we need to start, so after sunset everybody show up at the old Miller warehouse and get the paint you need to restore the color to your buildings. There are ladders and everything else you need to do this. We don't want anyone to see us, especially any reporters. But they're all gone anyway, so no problem there. We'll hit the plants with herbicides after we finish with the painting. I got gallons of it. See you around nine."

*   *   *

By midnight, several business owners, along with their families, employees, and volunteers were busy slathering paint on their edifices. As sunrise approached, everyone returned home exhausted. Hours later, when Havertown's retailers returned to their places of business, they were flabbergasted to find their nocturnal efforts had been for naught. The buildings appeared just as they had before the great color jump. The new paint had somehow not taken hold—indeed, there was no evidence that any had ever been applied to the aging surfaces of the main street's shops and outlets.

"What happened? What's going on?" blurted Harrison.

"This can't be. It's crazy. We painted all night," sighed the owner of Howey's Ice Cream Emporium.

"This will make a good headline, but I might as well add that the town is headed for default," said Curt Johnston.

Charlie Trevor said nothing. He just stood with fellow members of the Havertown Business Coalition shaking his head and moaning in despair.

"Ha!" shouted Amy Clark from across the street. "You idiots are finally displaying your true color. Green suits you."

Only when she spoke did the mayor and his cohorts realize that their skin color had changed.

#

Losing Touch

Lust is the fool's muse.
— Gunther Purdue

"In the grand scheme of time, we're really the same age," said Peter Mulberry to sixteen year-old Kathy Miranda, his daughter's babysitter. "So let's just enjoy this joint and do what naturally follows."

For a long time he had entertained the notion that the girl was coming on to him. Always standing so close to him and smiling at him suggestively. He was sure she was infatuated with him, and he was amused, indeed flattered, by her apparent interest.

"Okay," responded Kathy, slipping off her coat. "I'll tell my parents you got back late."

Peter had been attracted to the teen from the moment he had set eyes on her a year earlier. He had fantasized being intimate with her and felt like a pedophile for doing so. *What are you thinking, man? Jesus, she's just a kid!* he reminded himself, but he could not keep himself from imagining what it would be like to make love to her. Petite--not much taller than his eleven year-old daughter—she had a delectable bubble butt (he had come to think of her as "Little Kathy with the perfect assy"), well-formed breasts (equally bubblicious), a luxurious mane of auburn hair, intoxicatingly blue eyes, and the complexion of a Bartolini marble. She was every middle-aged man's forbidden dream.

Since his wife had left him months before for her female lover, Peter had not been intimate with another woman ... not that he'd been intimate with his former spouse in recent years.

"Bet you've done this before," said Peter, lighting a stick.

The two Stolis and glass of Zinfandel he'd downed at dinner were still with him but not to the extent they were on his drive home. He was thankful he had not been stopped for drunk driving, because he knew he was hardly driving in a straight line.

"Only once," replied Kathy, taking a deep toke.

What are you doing, you damn fool? Getting a kid high to get into her knickers, Peter the Pedo. That's who I am. Freakin' Peter the Pedo. Major sicko!" admonished the voice in his head. *Stop! Just stop, you perv!* But he could not. He was a captive to the desire, the absolute lust, she inspired in him.

Is Shelly asleep? he wondered. *She must be or Kathy would have said something,* he reasoned.

"Wow, I think I'm already high," observed the babysitter, suddenly leaning against him as if to stop herself from falling.

"Whoa, I guess you are," replied Peter, clutching her narrow waist.

Just making contact with her taut body caused an electrical charge to shoot through his loins. *Oh, my God, she's beautiful.*

"You're very pretty, but I'm sure everyone tells you that."

"Not really. Guys my age are such idiots. They don't know what to say … or *do*," said Katherine, smiling at him mischievously.

"Well, we older guys can be idiots, too, but we generally know *what* to do," said Peter, thinking: *If you knew what to do you wouldn't be doing this!*

＊   ＊   ＊

By the time the doobie had reached roach size, Peter was feeling a seriously enhanced buzz as well, but even in his stoned state he knew that Kathy qualified as totally wasted. She sat against him on the couch with her hand resting in his lap. Meanwhile, he had managed to liberate her left breast from her blouse. Then with only a slight effort he laid her back on the couch and unbuttoned the top of her jeans and slid them off. *Perv! Perv! Perv!*

"*Oh*," Kathy mumbled, and Peter wasn't sure whether it was a sound of protest or shared pleasure.

All he could think about was making love to her. The thought made his pulse quicken. Any reservations he had about consummating the act with the underage adolescent had been remanded to the hinterlands of his conscience. Despite several tries to appease his desire, her body resisted his advances.

"*Jesus, maybe she's a virgin*, he thought, and the idea both excited and repelled him. As he continued to press against her, she moaned as if in discomfort, and Peter abandoned the idea of breaching the obviously chaste young female. For several moments he drank in her exquisite form, and then when she moved, he decided to quickly dress her in the hope she would not know what he had done.

*   *   *

Once she was fully clad, he took a seat across from her. Within minutes she climbed from her stupor and stared at him sweetly.

"Did I fall asleep? Did you just come in, Mr. Mulberry?"

Thank you, God, thought Peter, nodding. "Yes, you were fast asleep, and I didn't want to disturb you."

"Sorry, I guess I better go," said Kathy, looking at her watch. "Wow, it's late."

As she rose, she grimaced and reached for her waist.

"What's the matter?" inquired Carl, nonplussed.

"I think I must have put my pan … ah, I mean my … you *know*, on backwards," said Kathy, attempting to adjust her under garment.

Following an awkward silence, Peter offered to escort her home.

It was less than two blocks to the babysitter's house, and during the walk Peter tried to determine if Kathy had any recollection of what had happened. Finally relieved that she did not, he handed her two twenty-dollar bills ... twice what he owed her.

"That's *too* much, Mr. Mulberry."

"Hey, a little bonus for being such an excellent babysitter. I really appreciate your willingness to come over on such short notice—last minute dinner with a client. It was an important one," said Peter.

"No problem. I'm always available ..." replied Kathy.

As she ran down the walkway to the front door of her house, Peter pondered the meaning of her parting comment. *What the hell was that? Maybe ...*

*   *   *

The next morning his daughter asked about his dinner meeting and he in turn asked about her evening with the babysitter.

"Okay, I guess."

"What do you mean, *you guess?*"

"I don't like Kathy, She's a ..."

"A what?"

"A slut," answered his daughter, her nose scrunched up.

"What are you talking about?" asked Peter, incredulously.

"I didn't want to tell you, but she's had a boy over. She told me not to tell you," confessed Shelly.

"How does that make her a slut?"

"I saw her do stuff with him last night,"

"Huh?"

"They were naked on the couch and he was touching her boobies. They were making these weird,

69

groaning sounds. They woke me up. They didn't see me though. He had a tattoo on his back. I think it was a dragon."

Suddenly a horrible thought occurred to Peter. *Had she seen him?*

"What else did you see?" he asked with trepidation.

"Nothing, I just went back to bed and went to sleep after they stopped making those stupid noises."

Thank you! Thank you! Thank you! hailed Peter's inner voice.

"Don't worry. We'll never have her babysit you again," he assured his daughter, patting her cheek.

*   *   *

After obsessing all day over what might have been with Kathy, Peter called her from his office and asked her to meet him at the nearby Holiday Inn. Her reply was not what he expected. It signaled the start of a life-altering nightmare.

"I'm telling my parents," she blurted, adding, "and I know you did something creepy to me when I was at your house."

#

The Big Day

But the days of golden dreams had perished.
— Emily Bronte

Mitch Connelly woke up excited about the day ahead. An advance copy of his first book, a crime mystery, was due to arrive from the publisher. His anticipation level had been building steadily since his manuscript had been accepted almost a year earlier by one of the better presses. It was one of his dreams come true. The other important dream he had already realized by marrying his college sweetheart. The whole thing was storybook, he thought. "Got the most beautiful girl on campus and now my book . . . oh my, God, my book!" he squealed and leapt from the bed. When he reached the kitchen, his wife, Jennifer, was already dressed for work and looking drop dead gorgeous.

"Coffee's ready, sleepy head."

"You're going to have to fight off the guys at the office looking like that. Just make sure you *do* fight them off," said Mitch, kissing Jennifer on the cheek and patting her behind.

"No problem with that. They know where I stand. Married to the best looking crime writer in the whole world."

Mitch gave her a second kiss. "Today is the *big* day! Hello Pulitzer Prize!" blurted Mitch.

"You need to gain some confidence, honey," joked Jennifer, reaching for her briefcase. "See you later, Robert B. Parker."

"Tonight we celebrate, so get home early, baby."

"I will," said Jennifer on her way to the door. "Wouldn't miss the chance to be seen with a famous author."

"Love you!" shouted Mitch, receiving the same shout-back.

*   *   *

Mitch readied himself for work but as he thought about it his mood began to darken. Teaching four English composition courses every semester to barely literate students at Last Chance Junior College—as he called Farpin State—had taken a toll on him. *These kids haven't got a clue, and if they did, they wouldn't pursue it. What a waste of a perfectly good Ph.D.*, he lamented. He was right, too. Most of the students simply didn't seem to care. The only consolation he derived from his eight years at the institution was that he had his summers free to write. "God, let it be a hit so I can get out of here!" he mumbled, as he pulled out of the driveway and headed for work.

The campus was fifteen minutes from the Connellys' house, an easy trip through winding and tree-lined streets. Mitch had used the drive to adjust his attitude for the challenges that awaited him. *What you're doing is important and necessary ... even a noble calling. They're really not bad kids, just not Rhodes Scholars*, he told himself in an attempt to exorcize the urge to tell his department chair what he really thought about the lowly institution of higher learning—*Place only exists to give parents someplace to dump their little morons*, he had been tempted to say on many occasions.

Ahead of him a school bus came to a stop to pick up a small girl standing on the opposite side of the street. But Mitch was lost in his thoughts of glory and fame. *This book could do it all. It's good, really good. The pre-pub reviews have been great. Maybe a movie will ...*

When he saw the stopped bus in front of him, its flashing lights didn't register their significance. He kept driving to pass it. Then the small child appeared in front of him, and it was too late to avoid hitting her.

"Oh, my God!" Mitch screamed, climbing from his reverie. He looked through his rearview mirror and saw the child lying on the street in front of the school bus, the driver and a hysterical parent running to her side. Mitch hit the brakes, but then the consequences of what he had just done struck him and he pressed the accelerator and sped away.

Jesus, they saw you! They saw my license plate. I'm dead. Everything is ruined. The book ... Jennifer. It's all gone. I'll go to jail. What about the kid? You didn't stop. Maybe you killed her. What are you doing, you stupid bastard? Go back ... go back!! Maybe you can help. But he didn't heed his own words. Instead he drove back home.

*   *   *

Mitch sat in the driveway, his mind swirling as the car engine ran. *Get away! Run! Go to some place where no one knows you. Hide!*

The sun crept behind heavy clouds causing the neighborhood to become as bleak as Mitch's thoughts.

Not without Jennifer. Never! What are you thinking, you frigging jerk? There is no escaping what happened ... what you did was unconscionable. Everything was going to be so great, too. Now it's all destroyed. After a few more desperate moments, Mitch climbed from the car. As he moved up the walkway, the door to his house swung open and Jennifer appeared, waving an object in her hand.

"How did you know to come back? I forgot my cell and returned for it. When I got here, the Fed Ex truck drove up. Look, it came early."

His dire thoughts consuming him, Mitch didn't grasp the meaning of his wife's words.

It's *Leaving the Scene ... your* book, honey! Your *book!*"

Mitch took the volume from her hand and tossed it into the street.

"What are you doing?" squealed Jennifer.

"Call the police," uttered Mitch, tears streaming down his face. "I have to report a crime."

Beat

I want to create wilderness out of empire.
— Gary Snyder

Dig it! There's Kerouac tapping out his jazz while Ginsburg howls for love in the next room and Cassady dances his chemical rhumba on the sidewalk. Here comes Burroughs sniffing out a morphine lunch and Corso with his vestal lady scatting for Ferlinghetti in his city of lights. *Yeah, man*!

#

Trans -Mission

And the elements once out of it, it transmigrates.
— Shakespeare

Channel 64 had been anxiously awaiting the delivery of its new million-watt transmitter from China for over a year. It had taken the remote Arizona public television station five years to win approval from the Federal Communications Commission to dramatically boost its signal. The powerful transmitter was unlike any of its predecessors. Its design required merely one fifth of the electrical power and space of most conventional transmitters. In addition to those very appealing features, the new Sangwon 507 Sky Blaster configured a broadcast signal that guaranteed non-interference with other stations. Indeed, that had been the basis for the FCC's approval.

When the transmitter arrived, Giles Bookwaller was elated. For him it was a wish come true. During the fifteen years he'd served as KXOP's chief engineer, he had battled to keep the station accessible in its most populated signal areas. Between the low power assigned by the FCC and the age of the transmitter, this was a formidable challenge for Bookwaller. The constant harping by the station manager, Bill Fableau, about the lousy reach of the signal kept him in a nearly constant funk. When he had come across an ad for the Sky Blaster in Broadcast Engineering, he felt it could be the answer he had been hoping for. What additionally excited Bookwaller was the transmitter's price. While it was not cheap—no television transmitter is—its remarkable features made it a bargain.

It took Bookwaller a while to convince Fableau to inaugurate a fundraiser for the transmitter and even longer to accumulate the pledges necessary to purchase it. When the station finally did, it then took even longer than expected to get it delivered. Now, as Bookwaller took apart the wood crate that had carried the new piece of equipment from the Far East, he joined the loud, churring calls of the Cactus Wren that were ubiquitous on the plateau—the site of KXOP's offices, studios, transmitter, and antenna.

"Whoa, there you are, you beautiful thing!" blurted Bookwaller at the first sight of the Sky Blaster. "Jeez, only about the size of my old desktop computer. Amazing!"

While he had seen its specs in the material sent to him by the Sky Master's manufacturer, its actual dimensions surprised him.

"You're about a fifth of the size of Big Bertha here," he said, nodding in the direction of the old transmitter. "And ten times more powerful. Those Chinese are remarkable. How do they do it?"

Despite a sudden severe and unseasonal lightning storm, Giles decided to fire up the new transmitter. He knew it was counterintuitive to test it during an atmospheric electrical disturbance, but he didn't want to wait any longer. To avoid disrupting the station's programming, he installed the Sky Blaster after the station signed off at midnight. By four in the morning, he had successfully tested the field strength of the new piece of equipment by calling station employees in far-flung locations of KXOP's signal area. The results were impressive. The station reached everyone loud and clear.

"Never got the station this good," proclaimed KXOP's receptionist, who lived the greatest distance from the antenna. "Whatever you did was magic, Giles. Gonna make a lot of folks happy around here. Want me to call my cousin in Safford to see if she can get the station up there?"

"Yeah, you do that, Helen, and call me right back."

The signal proved to be strong in Safford, a town that had never been reached by KXOP's previous signal.

"Hot dog!" bellowed Bookwaller, when he got the news. "Sky Blaster it is. It's going to change things big time."

The station was soon flooded with emails and calls from delighted viewers, and before the week was out KXOP's donor pool had nearly doubled. Bill Fableau was beside himself with joy and promised Bookwaller a salary increase.

"You sure did breathe new life into these old call letters, Giles. I thought for sure our days were numbered with old Big Bertha. This rights the sinking ship. I'd kiss you if you weren't so damn ugly."

*   *   *

However, on Monday of the following week, during KXOP's live broadcast of its "What's Up, Southern Arizona" morning show, something truly inexplicable happened. As cohost Marge Lebow was discussing the aesthetics of cactus floral arrangements, a man in his underwear appeared out of nowhere on the chair next to hers. It caused her to jump and strike her hand on the needles of a baby Ferocactus. A loud scream followed. John Cahill, Lebow's cohost, sat riveted to his seat, his eyes fixed on the unexpected guest.

"What ... how ... who?" sputtered Cahill, as the equally befuddled visitor gazed tentatively at his surroundings.

The half-naked man then stood up and ran around the studio, frantically looking for an exit. When he finally located one, he dashed into the desert howling like a coyote.

"What the fu ...! Did that just happen?" inquired the director in the control room. "Get the cops. Tell them there's a wacko running around the station. How the hell did he get in? The studio door is locked."

"Don't know. It was like he just appeared out of thin air," replied the audio technician.

Meanwhile, the hosts of "What's Up, Southern Arizona" sat frozen as their images were telecast to the viewing audience.

"Tell them they're still live!" shouted the director into his headset.

The floor manager jumped from his stupor and nodded. For the remaining fifteen minutes of the program, Lebow and Cahill pretended that calm and reason had been restored, but their inane dialog suggested otherwise.

"What in God's name happened?" inquired Fableau, who had seen the bizarre broadcast at home. "Was this naked guy hiding behind the chair, for chrissakes?"

"No!" protested Marge, still frazzled by the extraordinary event. "It was like magic. He just popped up next to me like he'd been beamed in from somewhere. The chair was empty one second and the next this man in boxer shorts was there. I don't think he even had any idea what had happened. Did they find him yet?"

"The cops are looking but so far nothing," replied Bookwaller.

"Just some kind of kook. Keep the studio door locked from now on."

"It *was* locked ... always is locked when we're live," replied the director.

"So, how the hell did he get in there?" snapped Fableau.

The response from viewers was nominal, most thinking it was just part of the show. A handful called the station wondering about the sudden materialization of the "underwear guy," as they called him, but no one was really disturbed by the incident. Nothing else out of the ordinary happened until the end of the week when four women suddenly issued forth in the middle of "Cooking Without Killing." Sally Franz, the show's host, was in the middle of a diatribe regarding the dangers of high cholesterol cake frosting when joined by the disoriented homemakers.

The women were quickly escorted out of the studio and two were treated for shock. Again, the police were called, but with no reasonable explanation for how they got there by either station personnel or the women themselves, they were merely sent home. Sally Franz was so shaken by the episode that she could not go on with her program. She promptly left the station, speculating that the studio was the site of some kind of demonic portal.

"Lord knows what it leads to or what else is going to shoot out of it," she shouted back to Bill Fableau when he asked her where she was going. "And don't expect me to return until it's thoroughly investigated!"

"Jesus, can things get any worse?" bellowed the station manager as the host of his most popular local program drove away.

Things eventually did get worse.

*   *   *

Three weeks passed with no further aberrant disruptions, and everyone at the station breathed easier, although the mystery about what had happened never left anyone's thoughts. Then the dreaded boom dropped. As KXOP was in the midst of conducting its semi-annual fundraising telethon, its phone bank volunteers suddenly found themselves being pushed aside by dozens of instantly appearing strangers. Before long, the station's main studio was overrun by people in all manner of dress and several in no clothes at all.

"Go to tape, Giles!" demanded Fableau. "This is insane!"

After the studio was cleared out, the flustered station manager met with his staff in an attempt to shed light on the outlandish happenings. No one, including Fableau, could imagine why people were materializing out of thin air during live broadcasts. But there were suggestions about how answers might be found. The station's program coordinator recommended that the station hire a paranormal investigator to probe the matter. Other staffers said the station should go off the air permanently because it was endangering the lives of its viewers by apparently pulling them from their homes to the studio.

"And most of these people are just disappearing after they show up here," offered Kitty Maynard, the receptionist.

It was during this discussion that Giles began to connect the Sky Blaster to the incomprehensible occurrences. *It's just been since it was put on line.* He decided to keep his suspicions to himself. The idea that the new transmitter was somehow responsible for transporting viewers to the station during live shows sounded too absurd.

When the station signed off at midnight, Giles attempted to open the transmitter to examine it, but its access panel would not budge. He decided to consult its specs, but they were not in the place he had filed them. *This is crazy*, he thought. *It's like Hal in 2001 Space Odyssey*, he mused with growing frustration. No matter what he did, he could not access the interior of the Sky Blaster.

The next morning, Giles told Fableau his theory about the transmitter.

"A teleporter like in *Star Trek*? Jesus, why would it be doing that? *How* could it be doing that?"

"I have no idea, and it's only a crazy theory. But how else can this stuff be explained? It only happens during live shows, so if we don't air any, we might be okay until this can be figured out."

"Everything has gone to hell anyway. The telethon is ruined. Cops, reporters, and ghost busters are all over the place."

"I tried to reach the Sangwon people in China, but my email bounced back. I couldn't reach them by phone either."

"Maybe we should just go dark until this thing is resolved. That's it. Gotta do it. Kill the signal ... now! This shit has to end," ordered Fableau.

"Are you sure, boss?

"Damn sure. Pull us off the air."

Giles went to the transmitter and pressed the off switch, but the Sky Blaster remained in operation. *What the .... He* pressed off again, and nothing happened. The signal continued unaffected. Holy crap! *Well, there's one way to take you down*, thought Giles going to the electrical circuit panel. He pressed the breaker connected to the transmitter but it would not move. *Son of a .... Okay, time to play hardball.* He then hit the master circuit and everything went dark, except the lights of the Sky Blaster's meters. *Shit, still on! How the hell ...?*

"What's going on, Giles?" shouted Fableau. "No power anywhere."

Giles pressed the master breaker, and the lights came back on.

"We got a big problem, Bill."

"What now?"

"The transmitter won't shut down. It's on auto pilot, and no matter what I do, it sends out a signal."

"You got to be kidding. Okay, we'll just put up the 'technical difficulties' slide. Screw it."

"We could disconnect the line to the transmitter," offered Giles.

"To hell with it. We'll just air the slide. Better than going dark anyway. You've got to go to that manufacturer in China. Get there fast as you can. Those bastards built this goddamn thing. They can figure out what the hell is going on."

*   *   *

Two days later, Giles arrived in Yinchuan, China. He grabbed a taxi to the address of the Sangwon factory. But when he arrived at the location, he was surprised to see only a vacant lot.

"No, no. This is the wrong address," he explained to the driver, who answered him in broken English.

"Yes, 4211 Tiancun Lu. Is place," replied the driver pointing to the paper in Gile's hand.

"Need Sangwon factory," said Giles. "This is not the Sangwon factory."

""Sangwon factory? No Sangwon factory in Yinchuan. No such place."

"There has to be."

"No ... *no* Sangwon factory here," responded the cabby, shaking his head.

"Okay, let me out here."

Giles walked down the street and found nothing at all that resembled a manufacturing building anywhere nearby. *Get another taxi. Try again. Maybe the guy was wrong or didn't understand me.* After several minutes, he managed to summon another taxi.

"I *need* to find the Sangwon factory, *please*. You know *where* it is?" he asked the driver in what was nearly a pleading voice.

After a long pause, he was told that there was no business by that name in Yinchuan. Giles was about to argue the point, but then decided to return to his hotel. *Maybe someone there knows where the factory is*, he thought, his level of anxiety rising. His concern would peak when the hotel desk clerk and the manager corroborated the taxi driver's words.

"See, nothing in business directory," said the manager holding a thick volume in his hands. "Live here all my life and no such Sangwon. Maybe have wrong city?"

Giles returned to his room and Googled the plant, but this time there was no listing. *No, this can't be happening. Sangwon existed. I had contact with them. We paid 'em. They sent the friggin' transmitter to us. What in God's creation is happening?* Contacts with nearby cities, and eventually the American embassy elicited the same results—no such factory existed.

Giles spent a sleepless night, and the next morning he flew home completely flustered. He was totally perplexed by his unsuccessful attempt to make a connection with the company that made the Sky Blaster transmitter. His email to Fableau was met with utter disbelief and rancor.

"Christ, Giles, you bought this damn thing. You knew them. What the hell is going on? Didn't you check their credentials?"

Giles had to admit that he never did any background checking on the company. Its website was tremendously impressive and contained many glowing customer testimonials on its products. Nor had he contacted any of his engineer colleagues about the manufacturer, satisfied as he was with its on-line storefront and other links that purported a positive relationship with Sangwon. *Shit, why didn't I? My bad! My goddamn bad!*

*   *   *

Giles retrieved his car from the Phoenix airport garage and began his nearly two-hour commute home. He planned to stop on his way in Taylor for lunch and check out KXOP TV's signal. Since he had landed he was unable to access his email, and his cellphone had mysteriously gone dead and would not take a charge. *Can anything else happen?* he wondered, fearing the answer.

As expected, the television at Daley's Café in Taylor was tuned to ESPN. He asked that it be switched to KXOP for a moment and was happily obliged. What he saw shocked him. The studio was filled with people moving trance-like from the main door to the fire exit—a seemingly never ending line. Giles asked to use the phone and dialed the station. There was an automated out-of-order message. Giles left without waiting for his cheeseburger.

Just a couple of miles outside of Taylor, Giles discovered something that made him almost swerve off the road. The station's antenna, which could always be seen twenty-miles away, did not appear on the horizon. He floored the accelerator and shot across the empty desert. *Holy shit!* he blurted, when he realized that the station building was no longer there. Indeed, nothing remained of the station site. No structures, parking lot, or antenna. No evidence on the ground to verify that anything had ever been there. There was nothing to be seen anywhere.

He drove into the nearby village and found it empty. His stomach churned and he felt light-headed. *This is worse than a nightmare,* he moaned. *Everyone is gone. How … how?* He sat staring at the ghost town around him and then drove to his house that sat on the hill above it. Exhausted and shaken, he just wanted to sleep. *Maybe I'll wake up and all this will just be a mad dream.* Ten hours later he woke up … in darkness. There was no electricity in his house.

Giles stood on his deck and looked in the direction of the Petrified Forest, some fifty-miles away. The small towns that checkered the desert no longer broke the solemn darkness with their soft lights.

The wind pressed hard against him as he took in the endless panoply of stars and planets. One object shone a hundred times brighter than any other. But when Giles blinked, it was gone.

\#

The Favor

The Delight that consumes the desire.
The desire that outruns the delight.
— Algernon Swinburne

Palm Gordon stepped out of his vintage Studebaker Golden Hawk. He adjusted his tie and shook out the wrinkles in his gabardine suit jacket. When the traffic cleared, he walked with intent to the other side of the street toward Mora's Café. He caught his image in the glass door as he pushed it open and it pleased him.

Inside the small eatery sat a handful of people sipping coffee and eating eggs.

"Hey, Palmy, where you been? Ain't seen you in a coon's age. You dodging the bail bondsmen?" inquired Sammy Flynn, his thick fist wrapped around a white cup.

"You get uglier every time I see you, Sammy. That on purpose? How you doing?" replied Palm, taking a stool at the counter next to his friend.

"I been better and I been worse."

"You look on the worse end this time."

"Getting over the flu. Had me on my back for a week. Crapped and barfed off ten pounds."

"Hell of a diet."

"You ought to try it, Palmy. You could use a fin off your gut and a saw buck off your ass."

"Keep your eyes off my ass or you're going to lose more than ten pounds, you frigging fruit."

"Nice talk, Palmy. You're a real gentleman."

"Yo, Mora, my love, you got any fresh Joe in this joint?"

"No, honey, you know we only serve week-old coffee here," replied the middle-aged woman hanging between the two swinging half-doors leading to the kitchen.

85

"Well, give me a cup of the mud, and I'll have some white … no, make it rye toast."

"Getting daring in your old age, Palm? You never ordered anything but white toast before you disappeared. Have a life-changing experience?"

"Naw, just thought I'd break out of my slump."

"Good for you. Change is great, but don't get too crazy. Tomorrow you'll want a scone or bran muffin, and we don't got them."

"Where's Mack?"

"He's back here," answered Mora, jerking her head toward the kitchen.

"Tell him I got to see him, sweetie. Would you?"

"Anything for you, Palmy. You know that."

"Yeah, right. Could you get me some coffee while you're at it?

"Anything else? I live to serve you."

"Well, now that you ask," said Palm, eyeing her vast breasts.

"In your dreams," shrugged Mora.

"Yeah, you're in them a lot, sugar," winked Palm.

"Hey Mack, the Boss of Beeker Street wants to see you. Put down your spatula for a minute and get out here."

Palm Gordon had come by his dubious nickname at eighteen when he stole three cars in one day from the busy thoroughfare. The locals admired him more for the two years he spent in prison than for his ability as an auto thief.

"Well, look what the cat dragged in. How you doing, Palm?" said Mack, emerging from the kitchen. The two men shook hands and went to a nearby booth.

"I'm surviving. What about you?"

"Prostate has me crazy, but otherwise, I'm existing."

"How's Sara?"

"She's doing fine. Better every day she don't see your ugly puss."

"Don't worry, I'm staying clear of your little girl, Mackie. She deserves better than me. That's for sure."

"Don't be so hard on yourself. It just didn't work out. Shit, I ain't held on to nobody since Mary died. She was the only one could put up with me."

"Yeah, Mary was a keeper. So was your kid, but I screwed up as usual."

"You did big time. Took her awhile, but she's back on her feet."

"Sorry."

"So what brings you back here? Thought you left Rochester for good."

"That was the plan. Look, Mackie, I need a favor."

"If I can do it, I'll do it. You know that. I owe you."

Loan sharks had threatened to break Mack's knees if he didn't pay off what he owed, and Palm had bailed him out.

"I'd be making hash from a wheel chair if it wasn't for you."

Palm detailed his favor to Mack.

"Jeez, Palm. That ain't gonna be easy. You know that. Little close to home."

"Hey, maybe it's too much to ask. Forget about it, Mackie."

"No, no! Let me figure it out. I'll do it if I can. You got a number I can reach you at?"

Palm gave Mack his cell number and left Mora's Café.

Shit, of all the Goddamn things to ask me to do. I could get in deep trouble for this, thought Mack. *But I owe him and got to make good.*

Two days later, Palm got a call from Mack telling him to meet him at Mora's.

"I did what you want, but it wasn't easy. And I don't feel good about it, I can tell you that," said Mack, handing a package to Palm.

"You know I appreciate it, Mackie. I needed it bad. Wouldn't have asked if I didn't. It's what brought me back to this burg. The craving had me nuts. And you were my only hope. No way I could get it on my own."

"So we're even now, right?"

"Yeah, you don't owe me a damn thing anymore."

"Well, I hope you enjoy my daughter's special apple cranberry strudel, because lying to her makes me feel like crap."

Palm held the foiled wrapped package close to his chest as he left the restaurant.

#

Continuum

*Some things continue even
when you think they've ended.*
— Christopher Weber

It was more difficult than usual for Felix Wiley to climb out of bed, not that it was ever easy at the hour he had to rise and face the world. But this time he felt unusually weighed down and listless, despite a solid night's sleep. *No dreams again,* he thought. This struck him as odd since he had always had a very active dream life. It had been a couple weeks since his last one, and he wondered why his sleeping hours had gone so blank, like snow on a vacant television channel. *Nothing there ... just nothing to watch,* he brooded. He missed the sojourns into his unconsciousness and wondered if his nocturnal projector had run out of film. The possibility upset him. Some of his best adventures had occurred while he was asleep.

On his way to the bathroom, Felix brushed against a mound of clothes on a chair. *What the ...?* They were his. For a moment he scanned the pile of shirts, pants, suits, and sport jackets attempting to figure out why they were there. Then he concluded that his wife was rearranging the bedroom closet. It was something she had done before. However, when he looked at the adjacent chair, it was empty. He wondered why his spouse's clothes were not stacked on it. *She's always into some project,* he surmised, continuing on his way to relieve himself as he prepared for another day at work.

Felix dressed quietly so as not to disturb his wife and went downstairs and into the kitchen. When he opened the refrigerator for orange juice he was struck by how packed it was. *Jeez, what the hell is all this stuff?* He lifted the plastic wrap from several dishes. *Casseroles ... all kinds of casseroles. Where'd they come from? Lara sure didn't make them.*

89

Following several long swigs of juice from the container—his lips and mouth were parched and his thirst deep—he left the kitchen. As soon as he entered the hall, he was accosted by a strong odor. *More flowery air fresheners. Never enough for her. The place smells like a damn florist shop.* As he passed the door to the living room, the heavy aroma grew stronger. *Whoa, that's a little much. C'mon, Lara. This is way excessive.*

Felix glanced at the moon as he pressed his car door opener. The dull yellow orb seemed to be scrutinizing him. *Hey, old chum, just you and me out here again while the normal world sleeps.* His thoughts then shifted to his upcoming retirement from the TV station where he had worked as an engineer for over forty years. *No more of these lonely early morning commutes. Thank, God! One month and I can sleep in forever,* he reminded himself, smiling at the thought.

Two miles into his drive he passed the local Knights of Columbus Hall where he had spent countless enjoyable evenings with fellow members. The message on its signboard gave him a jolt.

In Memory
Felix Wiley, 1955-2012

He pulled into the parking lot and stared at the sign. Then he looked at himself in the rearview mirror as if to verify his existence. *What is this ...?* After a few moments, it occurred to him that his K of C buddies had played a joke on him. "Those bastards," he mumbled, and began to chuckle. Over the years, he and his longtime chums had pulled many silly pranks on one another—water buckets above doors, pills in drinks to turn urine blue, fake insects in the food, cellophane wrap over commodes, greased car handles—but Felix had to admit this one was a genuine doozy. *Hard to top it, but I'll sure try,* he thought, moving the steering wheel in the direction of the soulless road.

*　　*　　*

Lara had hit the snooze button twice and now the clock radio blared unrelentingly until she managed to locate the *off* switch. She lay in bed for a moment longer staring at the recently installed ceiling fan and wondering if she should take another day off from work. *No, you need to go in. Buck up, old gal. It's no better here. Better to keep busy, she told herself*, rising slowly. On her way to the bathroom, she passed the chair stacked with her husband's clothes and gently ran her hand across one of his shirts.

After showering, she went to the kitchen and was surprised to see the orange juice carton on the counter. *Had she come down for a drink in the middle of the night? It was possible*, she thought. Her sleep had been fitful lately, and she had been up wandering the house at all hours.

She returned the juice container to the refrigerator and surveyed its contents. *Get rid of this stuff before it's a health hazard*, she told herself. But the idea of removing the aging comfort food caused what appetite she had to vanish. The pungent scent of decaying flowers drew her to the front room. *They're rotting like everything else.* For the next half-hour she removed the worst of the cut flowers and felt better for having done so. *Get rid of the reminders. Air out this place … air out your life, Lara. But how?* she despaired.

Lara grabbed her briefcase and left the house in a near gallop. She knew something was wrong as soon as she was outside. *Where's his car? It's gone. How …?* She looked up and down the street and then removed her cellphone from her purse and dialed 911.

"My husband's car is missing. Stolen, I think. It's not in my driveway. Not anywhere."

She was surprised by the response. "We have located the vehicle. An officer will be right over, ma'am."

Within fifteen minutes the doorbell rang, and two officers greeted her.

"The car is in the K of C parking lot, Mrs. Wiley. Doors were open and the engine was running. May we speak with Mr. Wiley?"

Lara drew a long breath and fought back tears. She turned toward the policeman with a hopeless expression.

"I wish you could, officer. He died two weeks ago."

#

St. Mary's Accident

Over active toilet seat
busy little life
sitting with her fingers crossed
wants to be a wife.

#

Doppleman's Double

For double my vision my eyes do see,
And a double vision is always with me.
— William Blake

The idea that everyone has a lookalike, a physical double, fascinated young Sam Doppleman and set a series of events in motion that would change his life. *Could there actually be another person out there who looks exactly like me?* he wondered, running his finger across the spider-shaped vascular birthmark that covered part of his left cheek. *If so, we are brothers … true brothers.* The notion excited him and prompted his long search on the Internet to find his mirror image.

After viewing thousands of pictures from every conceivable source, he finally found what he believed was his lookalike. His heartbeat quickened as he enlarged the photo of his seeming duplicate. At the bottom of it were the words: "Jacob Ganger of East Hamden, New Hampshire, was returned to the custody of his parents after being charged with bringing a gun to school."

Sam immediately Googled the name and got six hits, none of which matched the person possessing his unique facial stain. In fact, there was no further mention of his twin on any search engine. Next he launched a search for his clone's hometown and discovered that it was located just two hours north of Worcester, where he lived. *Great! I'll go up and check him out personally,* he thought excitedly. *This could be the start of a great friendship. How can he not connect with someone who looks like him, especially someone who has what he has on his face?*

Sam had long hoped to have a meaningful relationship with someone … anyone. As an only child he always felt lonely, and with his pronounced facial blemish, finding friends proved a real challenge. He had only one close friend in high school, Billy Canon, and he was as much an outcast as Sam, because of his crippling Lupus. That friendship had come to an abrupt and tragic end when his sixteen year-old companion accidently fell to his death on the stairs in his house. It left Sam inconsolable and once again feeling isolated.

Having discovered his double, Sam now felt renewed hope that he might meet someone that could genuinely relate to his world. *Would anyone with his disfigurement not appreciate what he felt?* Sam was convinced that finding Jacob Ganger would make a significant difference in his life—and perhaps that of his double—and he resolved to find him. With his objective in mind, he set out to change his fate the following Monday.

His plan upset his parents, who tried to dissuade him about pursuing what they felt would likely lead to more frustration and disappointment.

"Yes, we can see the similarity in your appearances," said Ann Doppleman examining the image of Jacob Ganger. "But he's a complete stranger who may have nothing in common with you."

Sam pointed to his birthmark. "He has this in common with me and that's a lot ... a whole lot."

"Son, I don't think you should just show up at this young man's house unannounced. Why don't you call him up first? Or send him a twit ... or *whatever* you call it."

"Text, dad. It's a *text*. I couldn't find anything on him. Just his house address, so I'm going to go see him. No big deal. I'll just introduce myself, and he'll see why I did," said Sam, touching his discolored cheek again.

"It sounds like he's got some issues. Taking a gun to school isn't very smart ... *or* sane."

"Maybe it was an accident or he just took it there to show a friend. He didn't do anything with it," replied Sam defensively.

"Well, call us when you get there, and be careful. You never know what you're getting into."

"Don't worry, you guys. I'm eighteen. Not a kid anymore," assured Sam, putting on his coat and taking his car keys from the pegboard in the kitchen.

"We will worry," replied his mother. "That's what parents *do*, honey."

Sam kissed his mother and hugged his father and bounded out of the door to his waiting Corolla, formerly owned by his recently deceased grandfather.

Two-and-a-quarter-hours later he entered the small village of East Hamden.

*   *   *

After thirty days in the Millbury Cove Psychiatric Center, Jacob was pleased to be home, but not for the reasons one might suspect. He hated the house that he had lived in since birth. It was not filled with good memories. Indeed, from Jacob's perspective, the opposite was true. His parents had never treated him with the kind of affection he craved. They pretended to care, but he was certain they didn't. He believed his tarnished face was a painful reminder that they had given life to something defective ... even ugly. Through the years he developed a profound resentment toward them. They had made him—brought him into the world—and were, he thought, repelled by what they made.

The kids at school were no better. They treated him like a freak or just plain avoided him. Every girl he had formed an interest in looked down on him, and every guy he tried to befriend treated him with cool reserve, if not explicit contempt. In junior high school they had given him a nickname—Boris. At first he thought it was funny that they called him a name he did not recognize, but then he discovered that it was the moniker of the actor that played

Frankenstein, and it crushed him. During the next several years of school he became a loner.

Jacob immersed himself in the fantasy world of video and online games and developed a reputation among his anonymous combatants as a fierce, if not ruthless, competitor. "I demolish them all. No one ever gets the better of me. Bam, bam, they're dead!" he boasted to his parents over dinner. "That's good," they mumbled, half-listening to their needy son, and he recognized their indifference. "Bam, bam," he muttered again, shooting them with his eyes.

*   *   *

"I'm looking for the home of Jacob Ganger," said Sam to a middle-aged woman sitting at a desk in the tax assessor's office in the East Hamden Town Hall. It was the first office he found as he entered the solemn brick building. When she looked up from her computer her expression became distorted.

"Jacob? What do you mean? You know where your house is."

"No, ma'am. I'm not Jacob. I'm his double. I live down in Worcester and came up to meet him."

"I don't have time to be playing games with you, mister. You've been in enough trouble already, and you shouldn't be coming in here acting like you're someone else," replied the woman," her firmness compromised by the look of anxiety in her eyes.

"Really, my name is Sam Doppleman. Here, this is my license," said Sam, handing it to her.

The woman looked at it and back to Sam. "I'll be darned. You sure could be his identical twin, except your voice is a little different, and your manner, too. Amazing."

"So do you know where he lives?"

"Sure I do. He's Alice and Howard Ganger's son. They're over on Russell Street. It's not far. Go down to the next light and take a left. That's Russell. They're at 142, only a couple blocks after the turn."

Thank you, ma'am," said Sam turning to leave.

"I'm not sure he's the kind of double you want to have, son."

"Just going to say hi," replied Sam on his way out of the office.

*   *   *

At the precise moment Sam climbed back into his car, Jacob was inflicting the last of several blows to the head of his father, whose wife lay nearby in a puddle of blood. "You *never* cared!" he screamed, throwing the murder weapon, a garden shovel, across the wood paneled dining room. He reached into his father's pocket and removed a set of keys. He then ran to his father's study and unlocked a tall walnut cabinet, removing several guns and boxes of ammo and placing them into a large leather case.

When Jacob returned to the dining room, the doorbell rang and he peeked out the window to the porch. A kid his age bearing a striking resemblance to him stood at the door. "What the ...?" For a moment Jacob wondered if his mind was playing tricks on him, and then he became convinced that his lookalike at the door was a police officer disguised as him to take him back to the Wacky House, as Jacob called it. He would make sure that would not happen.

After another ring of the bell, Jacob answered the door. The doubles stood face to face without uttering a word for several moments. Sam finally broke the awkward silence.

"I'm Sam Doppleman from Worcester. God, you really do look just like me. I wanted to meet you. Sorry I just showed up without any warning. I know it must be really weird."

Both young men unconsciously held their forefinger on their birthmark.

"Yeah, weird," said Jacob, who then invited Sam inside.

"Thanks," said Sam as he was escorted into the living room.

It was the last word he ever uttered. Jacob had crushed his skull with a fireplace poker.

"You do look like my twin, but you didn't fool me. Maybe you'll fool *them*."

Jacob removed the wallet from Sam's pocket. "I'm you now, and you're the poor dead me. Nice trade off."

He then grabbed the case with the guns and ammo, and headed out to the garage.

"World, watch out. Here I come," he muttered, as he drove away filled with raging purpose.

#

Infected

Physicians of the utmost fame
Were called at once, but when they came
They answered, as they took their fees,
'There is no cure for this disease.'
— Hilaire Belloc

It was a momentary lapse in judgment—a split second impulse with unfortunate consequences—that impelled Connor Hickman to breathe his germs into his wife's open mouth.

If she gets my bug we may not have to go to her parents' house, reasoned Connor, as he exhaled. The last thing he wanted to do was spend three days with his in-laws in upstate New York.

Only seconds after his thoughtless attempt to infect Clare Hickman, she sneezed. *Now I've done it. How stupid and selfish of me. You know she has a weak immune system.*

The next day Clare had a fever and felt achy all over.

"I think I caught your cold, honey," she informed Connor, without accusation. "Bound to happen when we're so close to each other."

Connor felt terrible. *Yes, maybe she* would *have gotten my cold anyway, but maybe* not *if I hadn't placed my bacteria on her lips.* He felt like a criminal for behaving so incorrigibly and chided himself for his unconscionable behavior. *Let me be the one who gets the most sick, dear God ... please.*

*   *   *

Two days later, he took his wife to their longtime doctor, who prescribed an antibiotic for what he termed a "nasty infection."

"Some really strange bug out there," observed Dr. Corman. "Making people feel real odd. Won't believe some of the things I've heard. Wildest symptoms."

"Like what?" Connor asked.

"Sorry, doctor-patient privilege. Can't say, but take my word for it. Most unusual."

"I hear off tune violins and then some things look real flat as if they've been pressed down by a big weight," commented Clare, out of the blue.

"Like *that*," responded Corman, looking at Clare. "Just lay low, take the pills, and drink lots of liquids. You should be better in a couple of days. You don't sound all that great yourself, Connor."

"Yeah, I've had something, but I feel pretty good. Maybe a little funny, but generally okay. She probably got this from me," replied Connor, sheepishly.

"It's possible. You never know. These things do jump from host to host, so proximity is a factor."

I knew it. I gave it to her. You're such a son-of-a-bitch. God, make her better, pleaded Connor to himself as they returned home.

By evening, Clare appeared improved, and Connor was thankful, but he still felt culpable for his wife's illness. *Why'd I do that?* he asked himself over and over, his sense of guilt undiminished.

*   *   *

What ground Clare had gained the night before, she had lost by the next morning. Her symptoms were twice what they had been and now she was vomiting. Connor called Dr. Corman, who advised taking her to the ER where he was presently on call.

"I don't like the sound of this, Connor. Get her here as soon as you can."

It took every ounce of energy Clare could muster to put her clothes on, and at one point she nearly fainted.

"You'll be okay, honey. They'll clear this thing right up," Connor told his wife as he deposited her into their car.

"You're so good to me, Connor. I'm so lucky."

Not that lucky. You have a creep for a husband. How could I have done this to you? The one person I love more than anything, and I deliberately make you sick. What's wrong with me? lamented Connor, his foot pressed hard against the accelerator.

Minutes after reaching the hospital in El Centro, Clare was undergoing a series of tests. Connor sat anxiously in the waiting room. Directly across from him was one of the loveliest women he had ever seen. While Connor mindlessly thumbed through a ragged and ancient *National Geographic*, he found he could not keep his eyes from drifting in her direction. To his surprise and considerable satisfaction, she glanced at him. Finally, he gathered the courage to speak to her.

"My wife is here with the bug ... or something."

"My husband, too," responded the woman, smiling beguilingly. "Guess it's the season."

"I suppose," replied Connor, returning her smile. "Just getting over the grip myself. Think my wife caught it from me."

*   *   *

For several more minutes they lingered in each other's warm gaze, and Connor felt his heart race.

"You look familiar. Do I know you?"

"Funny, I was just about to ask you the same thing. By the way, my name is Linda," replied the shapely brunette with piercing grey eyes.

"Connor ... Connor *Hickman*. Linda what?"

"Smith."

"Nice name," replied Connor, completely smitten.

"Yeah, *real* unique," laughed the captivating stranger.

"I mean *Linda*. Always *loved* that name. I had a crush on a Linda when I was little. In fact, she kind of looked like..."

The woman rose and took a seat next to Connor. Her perfume aroused him, causing a stir in his lower extremities.

"There's *something* about you ..." whispered Linda, feeling light-headed and giddy.

"Exactly how I feel. Like something is, *ah* ..." muttered Connor, the ground seeming to roll under his feet.

"Should we...?"

"Yes ... *yes* let's," said Connor, clutching her arm and standing tentatively.

"What about them?"

"Who?"

"You know ... them," said Linda, nodding in the direction of the emergency room doors.

"Oh, *them*. They're *sick*," said Connor matter-of-factly.

"Of *course*, I forgot," chuckled Linda.

The blissful couple clung to each other and made their way out of the hospital.

"Nice sunset," observed Linda pressing against Connor.

"I've never seen both suns look so beautiful," he agreed.

"Do you fly, Connor? I mean really high?"

"Yes ... *yes*, I do," he answered, extending his wings.

#

Shade

Peace be upon you, for you have persevered!
— The Quran

Twenty-six kilometers south of Errachidia, Morocco, along the Qued Ziz River of rock and sand, stood the modest clay dwelling of the Khalad family. For generations the Khalads had raised sheep to provide their meager living. It was the only life they knew, and while it was a hard one, they accepted it with dignity and grace. As the new millennium arrived, all that remained of their small clan were two elderly aunts and Youssef and Houda Khalad, who had sired Abu and Hafeza.

While eight-year-old Hafeza spent many happy hours sewing cloth into garments and stringing beads into bracelets, her brother devoted his free time to napping and daydreaming under the cool umbrella canopy of the Dragon's Blood Tree that stood atop a one-hundred-foot rise behind his house. It was the only tree visible to the horizon, and Abu revered it more than anything besides his family.

To the eleven-year-old, it possessed a special magic. Since he had been very small, he had referred to the solitary growth as *Kaa'ba*, which his father had told him was the sacred House of Allah. To young Abu, his tree was the most magnificent object in his small world—as grand as the Goulmima Oasis he had heard his Aunt Naima speak of on many occasions.

"There is a place long miles to the north that possesses cool blue waters and towering date trees. Camels take their fill and people bathe and rest there. It is true *Jannah*."

Abu had pictured the sanctuary many times as he sat in his special spot under his beloved tree. There, too, he recalled the stories that his father had often told him. They were full of clever donkeys, talking deer, and camels appearing from stone. Among his favorite tales was one about a miser whose planted gold is stolen and then replaced by a common stone. Another told of a carpenter who foolishly builds a house badly and then is forced to live in it as it crumbles around him. Every story from his father contained a lesson and left a great impression on Abu.

Apart from the stories he'd been told, Abu was fond of inventing his own. On occasion, at least in his imagination, the tree would assist him as he devised his tales.

"The running camel began to fly across the Sahara," added *Kaa'ba*, as Abu fancied a mythic dromedary that comes to the aid of a lost caravan.

"Praise to you!" responded Abu. "That is what he would most certainly do. Thank you, *Kaa'ba*."

*   *   *

It had become a growing concern of Abu's that his precious tree appeared to be leaning more and more as time passed. Its roots were shallow, and Abu feared it would one day topple.

"Please do not fall, *Kaa'ba*," pleaded Abu. "Hold fast to the sand. I could not bear your death."

As Abu started his descent to his house, he noticed the southern sky had darkened.

"An *haboob*! Beg you not push down *Kaa'ba* with your harsh winds," implored Abu to the approaching wall of sand.

"Come, Abu, we must prepare for the sand storm," advised his father, as he closed the shutter on the single window to the stone hut.

The Khalad family huddled in the dark as the sand seeped through the cracks in the walls and covered them and everything they owned. Just as Abu feared, the wind struck with ferocity.

"*Kaa'ba* will be taken!" blurted Abu, rising and dashing from the house.

"Abu, come back! You will surely perish!" shouted his distraught father, but Abu could not hear him as he fought his way through the battering sand to the top of the hill.

Abu wrapped his arms around the trunk of the tree hoping to keep it from toppling. He remained in the same position throughout the raging storm as it lashed him with its stinging sand. Hours passed and the winds finally subsided. Exhausted, Abu fell asleep, his arms still wrapped tightly around his beloved evergreen.

*　　*　　*

When the sky cleared, Youssef and Houda Khalad climbed the rocky mound in a desperate search of their son.

"The tree is still there," noted Youssef hopefully, looking upward in disbelief. "It has not fallen!"

When they arrived at the summit, they saw their sleeping son.

"Praise be!" cried Houda, in great relief. "The tree saved Abu."

"Perhaps *he* saved the tree," replied Youssef, as Abu stirred from his dreams.

"Father, mother!" he shouted. "Look, *Kaa'ba* still stands, and the soil now covers its roots."

Indeed, the earth at the base of the *Dracaena cinnabari* had been built up by the blowing soil, and it now appeared to have a strong foundation.

"It's a miracle," muttered Abu, as he accompanied his parents down the hill.

When they reached the bottom, they noticed with great surprise and delight that the tree's previously limited and precious shade now spread across their hut.

"A miracle, indeed!" proclaimed the Khalads, gazing up admiringly at their son's cherished companion.

#

Those goddamn sneaky spies
with their sixteen millimeter eyes

In all the bathrooms of the world
little cameras *hummmm*
as they reel us in frame by frame
recording our hand
and bowel movements.

#

With the Push of a Button

There is no armour against fate.
— James Shirley

Don Tamely never thought he would love anyone as much as he did his daughter, although she could be a bit difficult at times. He was wrong. His affection for his grandson filled his heart as profoundly as had his love for his only child. While board games, shopping, and movies were the favored pastimes of Melanie Tamely, rough housing, sports, and video games were the passions of his nine year-old grandson, Toby. He recalled fondly the long-ago activities with his daughter but had to admit that he enjoyed the more physically rigorous pursuits with his grandkid. At times they raised so much of a raucous wrestling and carousing that his daughter scolded him as if he were a youngster as well. Indeed, Toby thought of his grandfather as more of a playmate than his mom's father. That suited Don because he knew it was the glue that so tightly bonded them.

"C'mon, papa. Let's fight," shouted Toby at the sight of his granddad, and Don would raise his fists in mock threat.

"I'm coming to knock your block off, so you better run for the hills," was Don's melodramatic rejoinder, and his grandson would let out an ear-splitting squeal and desperately seek a hiding place.

"Okay, papa, let's bring it down a few clicks," appealed Melanie, giving him a kiss on the cheek.

"Sure, sweetie, we'll try to behave."

"How about a game of checkers or monopoly with Toby? Something low key for a change."

"Checkers? No, we're going to play Samurai warriors. But we'll keep the noise at a reasonable level. Come out, you ninja and face your master," growled Don, moving in the direction of his grandson's usual hiding place behind the couch.

It wasn't long before Melanie was pleading with them to chill out, and by that time Don was feeling a bit spent anyway.

"Okay, sport, let's surrender our arms for the day. How about an ice cream?"

"Yeah!" shouted Toby at the top of his lungs.

"Fine . . . fine. Go get some ice cream but have him back by eight. It's a school night, dad."

"You got it, honey. Let's go, Miyamoto. Off to DQ."

"Who's Miya . . . ?"

"*Mi-ya-mo-to Mu-sa-shi.* He's the greatest samurai of them all. You remind me of him."

"Really, papa?"

"Well, you sure can handle a sword like him."

"Yay!" squealed Toby. I'm Miyamushi!"

"That you are, my fearless warrior. That you are."

*   *   *

On the return ride home, Don asked Toby what he wanted for his upcoming birthday.

"Naughty Children?"

"Huh? What's that?"

"A video game."

"Oh, what kind?"

Toby giggled. "It's fun. You do funny things to parents."

"What kind of funny things?"

"Oh, . . . you make them mad."

"Why?"

"Cause you trick them."

"How?"

"You slime them when they try to punish you."

"Hmm, I don't think that's very nice."

"And you make them fall in the mud when they chase you. But they don't get hurt."

"Well, I hope not."

"You put them in jail when they yell at you. And you can have a dragon chase them with fire. He doesn't catch them though. It's so fun, papa. Will you get it for me?"

"I'll ask your mom."

"She doesn't like it."

"I can surely understand why."

"Please, papa. I really, *really* want it. It's not a bad game."

"I don't know. I think your mom will get mad if I do."

"No, she won't. It's what I want the most, papa. Please!"

"Well, I'll think about it."

"You can get it online. The stores don't have it."

"Maybe there's a reason for that. They don't want to anger parents."

"It's not bad. Honest, papa. You'll see."

*   *   *

That evening, after eating his supper, Don went to his computer and did a search for Naughty Children. It was the first link on the page that came up and he accessed it. The site featured two smiling children and the words, "Adults Only." *That's weird*, he thought, clicking the disclaimer to gain entrance. What he saw shocked and disgusted him. The same children on the site's initial page were engaged in a lewd sexual act. Don went to hit the exit button on his keyboard but inadvertently struck the download key. *Oh, God. What the hell did I do?* he thought, panicking. *Get off of this page now! Hit the back arrow.* Nothing happened. In desperation Don pulled the plug from the surge protector. *Dammit! That can't be the right url. What's going on? A kiddie porn site? Jesus! Did Toby go on it?* After a couple of minutes, Don restarted his computer and held his breath while it booted up. *Thank, God,* he thought, as his normal desktop appeared, without the X-rated site.

Once again he did a search for Naughty Children and carefully scanned the page that filled the screen. Just below the link he had originally accessed was one called "Naughty Children Games." *Aha, let's hope* ... With trepidation he pressed the cursor, and to his measurable relief it was, indeed, a site featuring the video game Toby wanted. Don quickly ordered it and went off-line to watch the Tigers take on the Red Sox. By the seventh inning stretch, he could not keep his eyes open, and he retired for the night.

The ringing of the doorbell, followed by several hard knocks on the door, awakened him.

"Mr. Tamely, open the door now! This is the police!"

Don immediately feared something had happened to his daughter or grandson. He threw on his robe and dashed to the front door.

"Mr. Tamely, we have a warrant for your arrest for attempting to obtain Internet child pornography. You have the ..."

"What are you talking about?" demanded Don as the officer read him his Rights.

"Last night an Internet watchdog group, called the Canadian Child Cyber Protection League, conducted a routine sweep of area computer use and found that you attempted to purchase child pornography, Mr. Tamely."

Oh, Christ, the download ... I hit the goddamn download button! recalled Don, his heart rate accelerating.

"It was a mistake, officer. I was trying to buy my grandson a video game and ended up on this awful site.

When I tried to leave it, I hit the wrong key, but I unplugged my computer right away."

"You'll have to come with us, Mr. Tamely."

"You mean I'm under arrest?"

"Yes, sir. You may call your attorney at the station."

Don was handcuffed and led to the waiting police car.

"This is a horrible mix up. I would never look at something so repulsive. I have a nine-year-old grandson, for God's sake!" protested Don as the vehicle sped away.

*   *   *

By the time Don was released from jail later that day, pending a court date, the media had picked up on his arrest. It was during the evening newscast that his daughter heard about it. Stunned, she immediately called her father.

"It's all a terrible blunder. I was trying to order a video game for Toby, and I got this terrible kiddie porn site."

"What video, dad?"

"It's called Naughty Children."

"I don't want him to have that. It's demeaning to parents and gives kids the wrong ideas," said Melanie, as if that was the reason he had been arrested.

"No ... no. It wasn't for *that*. Like I told you, I ended up on this ..." Don sighed in exasperation. "Look, why don't I come over and explain the whole thing in person?"

"You were on a child pornography site?"

"By accident, yes. I'll come over."

"No, dad, I don't think you'd better until all of this is cleared up. Toby will hear about it, and he'll be confused as to why his grandfather was arrested. Besides, didn't they order you to stay away from children until after your hearing? That's what they said on TV."

Don remembered that he had, indeed, been told to stay away from kids, and his heart sank again. As he spoke, his voice cracked and he swallowed hard to prevent a tearful wail.

"He's my grandson. You know this is all a horrible mistake. For heaven's sake, Melanie, do you doubt it?"

There was a slight pause before his daughter answered.

"Well, I'm sure you didn't mean to download that disgusting stuff."

"Jesus, I hope you believe that, Melanie. This is the worst thing that ever happened to me. Everybody is going to think I'm some kind of pedophile. How will I show my face in the community? I can't believe this is happening. Please explain the mistake to Toby so he doesn't think his papa is some kind of freak."

"I will, dad. I have to go now. We'll talk tomorrow, okay?"

*   *   *

Don's phone did not ring again for three days, and he was unable to reach his daughter, leaving message after message. He resisted the idea of driving to her house or for that matter going out at all. He just couldn't deal with people's disapproving looks, which is what he was certain he'd encounter. After the long silence, the phone finally did ring, but it was his attorney conveying that his hearing had been moved up to the next day.

"Don't worry. They know these things can happen, and you have no record of child ..."

"Porn?" said Don, sarcastically.

"Everything will be cleared up tomorrow. Take it easy."

"I'm going to be stigmatized forever by these awful accusations. You know that. People will always wonder if I *am* a pedophile. Once the claim is made, you can never fully erase it. That's a tragic fact."

"Sorry, Don, really. Just be at the courthouse at nine in the morning, all right? Things will get better. Trust me."

As Don's lawyer had predicted, the charges were dropped. Melanie had shown up for the hearing and was relieved by the outcome.

"Maybe you should go away for a while until things settle down, Dad."

"Naw, I'd rather hang out with Toby. Maybe take him to Niagara Falls, like we always planned."

"I think it would be better for him if you stayed away for a while, maybe a month or two," said Melanie, looking away from her father.

"What? You got to be kidding. What's going on? You're acting like . . . well shit, like I'm *guilty*."

"No, Dad. Don't be silly. Of course, I don't believe that. Why would I? You never did anything to me when I was little."

"Yeah, Melanie, why *would* you think anything but good thoughts about me?"

"Look, Dad, take a vacation, and when you get back, you and Toby can pick up where you left off . . . *please?*"

∗ ∗ ∗

Four days later, Don sat in silence on the terrace of his room at a Ramada Inn in Honolulu. It was a return to where he and his deceased wife had spent their last vacation. He watched the sun sink into the emerald surf and gently vanish. *Things will never be right again*, he reflected mournfully, allowing his tears to gather in his beard. *Just never be the same . . .*

Secrets of the Saints

From all the deceits of the world,
Good Lord, deliver us.
— Prayer Book

Two sentences on Marligold College stationary altered the course of Ah Sook Pae's life forever.

The Promotion and Tenure Committee has decided against your application for tenure. Your contract with the university will expire at the conclusion of the forthcoming academic year.

The young woman's first reaction was one of disbelief. *Who's playing this nasty joke on me?* she wondered, half chuckling.

Ah Sook inspected the envelope the letter came in. It looked official. Her heart suddenly sank. *No, this can't be real. They must have gotten my name mixed up with someone else's. I did everything I was supposed to do. Everyone told me I was sure to get tenure. This just makes no sense. It's crazy.*

She reread the short missive yet again. *That's all? No explanation? After all I went through, this is all they have to say? Impossible!*

Hoping it was a horrible mistake, Ah Sook called her department chairperson, Millie Haywood.

"I'm very sorry, Ah Sook. I just found out from the dean."

"I don't understand. I had everything required— tons of publications, good student and peer evaluations, department and university service ... What can I do? This is a nightmare," said Ah Sook, her voice cracking.

"There is an appeal process. Make an appointment with the academic vice president. He should be able to give you an idea of why the vote went against you."

Ah Sook couldn't hold back tears and barely managed to choke out a sentence.

"Can ... *can* he reverse the decision?"

"It's been done, but I don't think Kline has reversed such a decision since coming to Marligold."

"Did anyone in our department vote against me? Why would anyone do that? I know the junior faculty was behind me. I thought the senior faculty was, too. I was friendly with everyone. Nobody seemed unhappy with me."

"Sorry, I can't reveal the vote, Ah Sook, but I know you were well-liked and respected by us."

"Then why would the Tenure Committee do this?"

"You can never tell what they're looking at. Remember, we lack the larger context with which they are dealing."

"My file was the best the department had ever seen. Remember what everyone said in the faculty meeting?"

"It was exceptional, Ah Sook. You have nothing in your record to feel bad about."

"How can I *not* feel bad when I have been turned down for tenure? My career is irreparably damaged now. It's a black mark against me that will never go away," blurted Ah Sook into her cellphone.

"I'd make an appointment with the AVP. It might give you some insight, Ah Sook. I'm really sorry. This is understandably very upsetting to you, I know."

"I worked so hard for this, Millie. For six years my life has been all about getting tenure. I don't know what to do now. I'm devastated."

Ah Sook could tell from the silence emanating from the other end of the receiver that her department head had nothing further to say—that she had said all she could or was willing to convey on the subject. After an awkward pause, Haywood suggested that they have lunch the following week and Ah Sook agreed.

*　　*　　*

Staring out of her apartment window at the gray landscape, Ah Sook contemplated her next move. *How can I tell my parents in Korea?* she wondered, her anxiety surging. *They will be so disappointed and wonder why I failed. I did not do enough, they will think. But I did ... I did. Was there something I missed?*

Tears filled her eyes, distorting the view outside. *Everything seemed so good. Now my life is ruined. I'm humiliated. How can I show my face to my friends and family? I don't understand ... I just don't get it!*

Ah Sook slumped in a chair and cried herself to sleep. It was dark in her apartment when she awoke. Her tenure denial struck her immediately, and she resisted the urge to scream and throw something. "Why ... *why?*" she muttered but then could not contain her raw emotions. "Fuck them! Fuck them!" she shouted. "They can't do this to me!" *But they have ... they have*, she thought, feeling totally forlorn and defeated. *I wish I would die. There's nothing left.*

Two days later she had to appear on campus to teach her classes. She did so with a mix of trepidation and mounting anger. She knew that her colleagues would have heard about the tenure decision. Word on something like this always got out. For weeks people had asked her if she'd heard anything, and invariably the other junior faculty assured her that she had tenure in the bag. They were so eager for her. Now she would have to respond with her embarrassing news, and she dreaded the reactions she knew she would get. The last thing she wanted at this point was sympathy ... anything but. What she wanted was a clear explanation from the administration—the dean and academic vice president. After hearing from them, she would decide whether to appeal the decision of the Tenure Committee.

Rather than head directly to her office, she decided to talk with her closest colleague in the department, Mary Connors, about the disaster that had befallen her.

"Oh, my God! That can't be true. How could they? I'm so sorry, Ah Sook. What can you do? Are you going to appeal? You must. This is completely unfair."

A similar reaction came from two other colleagues, and then it was time for her to meet with her class. The very idea now seemed like an additional cruelty. She loved teaching, and now that was about to be taken from her. As soon as she entered the classroom, she broke down and had to leave. Her students were left baffled and concerned, and when two asked the department chair what was wrong, they were told she had received some upsetting news. But Haywood could not and would not elaborate on what that news was.

By the end of the day, word about Ah Sook's bad fortune had spread throughout the department. The news appeared to upset and puzzle everyone. That someone so obviously entitled to a positive outcome from the Tenure Committee could be turned down raised disturbing questions in the minds of other tenure-track faculty about their own prospects for achieving tenure at Marligold.

*   *   *

Ah Sook's meetings with the dean and AVP only compounded her frustration and deepened her depression. Both had told her that the Promotion and Tenure Committee was dissatisfied with the direction of her research and her inability to secure grants. They did not elaborate on the former, indicating that the latter was extremely important for faculty at a school seeking top tier status among elite institutions of higher learning.

"Our mission is to achieve parity with Research 1 institutions. To achieve that, we must bring in at least $40 million in annual federal support. The Tenure Committee did not believe your work was likely to generate meaningful funding," explained the AVP, Don Morrow, impassively.

Ah Sook countered that it was difficult, if not impossible, in her particular field of research to obtain grants—that few avenues of research support existed in the discipline of rhetorical studies. It was a known fact amongst her Communication Department colleagues when she was hired. Her protest received no measure of appreciation or understanding, and realizing this, Ah Sook excused herself, turning her back on the AVP's extended hand.

"Well, I'm sure you'll find a place that fits your estimable talents," said Morrow, as Ah Sook quickly left his office.

Despite the strong urging of her colleagues, Ah Sook decided not to pursue an appeal. Everything she had heard had convinced her that doing so would not change her fate and might just provide the institution with further opportunity to demean her. Moreover, conversations with other members of the department led her to suspect that someone among her own senior faculty had raised concerns about her. What they might have been, nobody could imagine.

Why would anyone in the department do this? They know there's no funding in rhetorical research, if that's the criticism. None of them have received grants either. And they never mentioned this in my fourth year review. Why was someone here out to get me?

Ah Sook obsessed over the issue in the days that followed. The only answer she could come up with was that they were actually envious of her substantial productivity because they did virtually no publishing themselves. Her suspicion was corroborated when a contract member of the department, Cary McCormick, expressed his view that a certain senior faculty had also blocked him when he sought to have his position converted to a tenure-track line.

"The old cadre here think they're the saints, the holy order, of the department, and they don't want anyone to draw a breath from their rarified air, especially not those who might make them appear unworthy of their lofty status or head the department someday. They made tenure when Marligold was a very different place, a lowly commuter college, with no ambitions to join the hallowed ranks of research institutions. Not one of them would get tenure in this school today. They do so little, and what they do is third rate. Yet they sit in judgment of those of us who do genuine scholarship, and they assassinate anyone they perceive as a threat to their hold on the status quo."

"You really think one or more of the senior members went against me? That there's this cabal against anyone who works hard and gets recognition in their field?" asked Ah Sook, feeling her entire body stiffen.

"That would be my informed view. What else? I've seen it happen many times before. They anoint those who share their mediocrity and eliminate those who defy it. Cornwall is the worst, too. Look what he's done over the decades he's been here. Maybe two pubs and those in second tier journals."

"But he's so friendly. Always comes into my office and talks to me. Acts like a mentor. I can't believe he would vote against me," replied Ah Sook, looking at the floor.

"That's his game—seduce and slay. I'm sorry, Ah Sook. You deserved better, like so many others. Do yourself a favor and get out of here. Have you been interviewing?"

Ah Sook sheepishly admitted that she had not even applied elsewhere because she had been certain she would be granted tenure at the college.

"I was blind, I guess. I never saw anything but a positive outcome."

"They lulled you into a false sense of security. That's their technique. When they see that someone has the potential to outshine them and possibly lead the unit, they scheme their demise."

"I feel so stupid … so naive," responded Ah Sook, tears beginning to stream down her face again.

"You aren't. You were just a trusting person in a place where that is a very *bad* mistake," said McCormick, handing her a tissue.

Ah Sook thanked him for his views on the matter and then cancelled her last class of the day. She felt hollowed out and highly agitated and didn't want to face her students in that condition. She cared for her students. They deserved more, too.

*   *   *

It was just as she had thought. Her parents, who had always pressured her to perform at the highest level, did not understand why she was refused tenure. Rather than consider that she might have been cheated of a just outcome, they assumed the decision was due to her failure to meet the standards established for gaining tenure. From their old world perspective, institutions were always in the right. The Paes recommended that their daughter return home and seek a husband. That was something she could not conceive of doing, but in order to avoid further displeasing her parents she did not raise objections.

By the time the conversation ended, Ah Sook was nauseous and trembling. She had not experienced such a sense of hopelessness since the year before, when her boyfriend of three years had fallen for another woman and ended their relationship. Even then she had had her career to keep her from going under completely. Now she had nothing to hold onto and felt as if she were sinking in a bottomless sea.

Ah Sook's lunch with her department chair did not improve her dark mood. To the contrary, if anything, it deepened it. Haywood's unwillingness to reveal any information about the senior vote and her growing coolness convinced Ah Sook that the roots of her trouble existed in her department and extended from there to the Tenure

Committee. This view fanned her rising hostility toward the senior faculty and administration alike.

"So, you're not going to appeal the decision, Ah Sook? That's probably smart. It may spare you more unhappiness," observed Haywood.

"I couldn't be more *un*happy with this place if I tried. But I've become convinced that it will do me no good at all to throw myself at the mercy of the Marligold hierarchy. There's clearly little compassion in the hearts of *certain* people."

Ah Sook gave Haywood a harsh look and excused herself, pushing her half-eaten salad aside as she rose from the table to leave the restaurant.

*   *   *

Later in her apartment, Ah Sook reviewed her years at the college looking for anything that might reveal a gap or breakdown in her performance. *Would they have acted against me without a legitimate reason?* Her self-doubt coupled with her suspicion about the motives behind the college's decision to terminate her made it increasingly difficult for her to function normally. She took to her bed for several days, prompting the department secretary, Betty Sampson, to phone and email her numerous times until Ah Sook finally responded.

"Are you all right?" asked Sampson. "I heard about what happened, and I'm so amazed and upset by it. How can I help? Do you need anything?"

"Thank you for calling," answered Ah Sook meekly. "I'm just having a hard time right now, but I'll be in tomorrow."

"Do you want me to get you anything? I can drop by your house. Maybe you need company?"

"Oh no, but thank you, Betty. That's very sweet. You're so kind. I'll see you in the morning."

Ah Sook did meet with her classes the next day without breaking down. She offered no explanation about her previous behavior to her curious students, but it was soon apparent to them that something was terribly amiss with their professor. After taking attendance she launched into a rant about the treachery of duplicitous communication.

"Be careful of false rhetoric. You cannot always believe what people say. Behind words often lies deceit. You've heard it said that people often say one thing and then do another? Well, I can tell you that that is something I have experienced first hand at Marligold. Do not be led astray by hollow and contrived expressions of friendship and approval. Understand that there exists ill will in many people, and it is shrewdly disguised in all forms of mock geniality ...

Ah Sook's verbal tirade lasted half of the allotted period, and she dismissed the class without addressing student questions. She repeated the same cautionary diatribe in her next class. At the conclusion of her teaching day, she felt satisfied that she had alerted her students about the rampant deceit that she had recently come to believe existed in human nature—more than hinting that it was present in alarming abundance among the institution's upper echelon.

*   *   *

As the semester came to an end, Ah Sook's mood had eroded further. She had distanced herself from everyone in the department, including those who had been closest to her. She had also isolated herself from the few friends she had outside of the institution. Given her single-minded pursuit of tenure since arriving in the area, her social life had been virtually non-existent, and following the breakup with her boyfriend, she had devoted all of her time to research and publication.

In her seclusion she grew more and more morose, at once deriding herself for failing to succeed at Marligold and then condemning those she perceived as the cause of her failure. Soon she stopped responding to all attempts to communicate with her.

"You're a loser! Pathetic! Just nothing! Better off dead!" she spat at her image in the bathroom mirror.

Upon closely examining her reflection, Ah Sook beheld a haggard figure. Her youth was gone, leaving behind the dire effects of despair and remorse.

"You don't deserve to live," she whimpered. "What good are you?"

In the middle of the night, she woke with a start, hearing loud voices outside of her window.

"Ah Sook is not good enough," proclaimed a familiar voice.

"She is inadequate," declared another.

"Subpar," agreed a third.

Ah Sook moved to the window and peeked out. In the glow of the streetlight stood Haywood, Cornwall, as well as the dean and the academic vice president. She gasped as their faces took on grotesque characteristics.

"Inadequate! Not good enough! Subpar!" they chanted as they morphed into hideous monsters.

"No!" screamed Ah Sook, closing the window and drawing the curtains.

She ran to her computer and tapped its keys frantically. On the screen appeared a list of local gun shops.

#

And he cried, *bring it on*!

I think about that someone
who I will never see again.
— Malcolm McKinney

The loss of the deeply beloved ... God, what it does to the soul! Clive was devastated by the death of Sara, his once and forever lover. She was alive one instant and gone the next. *Is there any greater cruelty? Could life impart a more excruciating kind of pain,* he wondered? *No, how could it?* He knew he would never get over the hurt. But he did not want to. That would mean diminishing what she meant to him, which was everything—the gathered molecules of the universe, the length and breadth of space. No price was too great to keep her vivid in his mind and heart. And he was good with that. *Damn* good with that.

#

The Cloud

Ye can discern the face of the sky.
— St. Matthew

It had been there for most of his thirty-seven years. A small cloud had appeared in the sky directly above Dennis Moore when he was little more than a toddler. At first, he didn't question why the same white puff was always hovering above him. But when he was about to enter kindergarten, he asked his mother what it was. She looked up to where her son was pointing and said, "What, you mean the sun? You shouldn't look directly at it, honey. It can damage you eyes."

"How come it's always there?" he asked.

"The sun isn't always in the sky. Sometimes it's cloudy and they cover it … but not today. There's nothing but blue skies, like the song says. Wish it would last."

Dennis could not recall there ever being a day when the same little plume wasn't hanging over him. It seemed to follow him wherever he went. As he got older he could not figure out why it cast no shadow like other airborne objects did. On several occasions he asked his friends if they could see the cloud, and he was always disappointed and frustrated when they responded negatively.

"You got clouds in your eyes, Dennis," was a familiar refrain, as his friends reacted to his frequent inquiry.

"What shape is it?" he was asked, even though his playmates could not see what he claimed to see.

"I don't know. Like a … *cloud*," he would answer, exasperated that he could not discern any particular design in the omnipresent object. "It's just kind of fluffy, like a piece of cotton."

As the years progressed, the cloud remained fixed and intact. Dennis was pretty sure he could even see it at night. He talked about it often—to the growing concern of his parents. Finally, they had his eyes checked, but testing revealed no impairment in his vision. When he persisted in his claim about the stalking nebula, he was sent to a child psychologist. After several visits, however, the therapist could find nothing abnormal in his behavior.

"Children sometimes create these things, like invisible friends, for mostly innocuous reasons. He'll outgrow it. Just play along with him and don't make an issue over it," advised the doctor.

Eventually, Dennis stopped mentioning the apparition because he could see the negative impact it was having on his parents and the increasing teasing it inspired in his playmates. Yet, he never stopped wondering what it meant or if it possessed particular significance.

*   *   *

By his early teens, he began to perceive images in the cloud's shape. The closer he examined it, the more it revealed an array of disquieting forms—menacing animals, gruesome faces, claw-like limbs, and so forth. On these occasions, Dennis would desperately try to avoid looking up, but something always seemed to draw his attention skyward. To his relief, there were times when the shapes appeared more benign ... even pleasant. The most frequent among these happier manifestations were an angel and a racecar. He favored the latter, since it was his fondest boyhood dream to become an Indy champion.

By the time he was married, he had taken the ever-present overhead object for granted. On occasions when he did look at the cloud, he was relieved to see that it no longer resembled anything other than the nebulous wisp that it had been originally. But he never forgot that it was something only he could see. By the time his own son was born, Dennis had accepted the cloud as a permanent product of his mind's eye—a phantasm that would never fade away.

But one day it did.

When he brought his wife and newborn home, he noticed that the cloud was gone. It took him by such surprise that he froze as he was opening the car door for his wife.

"What's the matter, Dennis?"

"It's gone."

"What's gone?"

"The cloud."

"Huh?"

He had never revealed his persistent and bizarre vision to his wife, and he caught himself before doing so. He knew it would only open a difficult discussion.

"The clouds ... it's really clear. There's no, *ah* ... clouds," he sputtered.

"Yes, it's a perfect day," she replied, beaming as she gathered up their infant from the bassinet on the backseat.

*   *   *

At first the sudden disappearance of the cloud filled Dennis with relief, but slowly its absence began to weigh on him. He felt as if he'd lost a limb, and he became so consumed by the sensation that he was nearly oblivious to what was happening around him—foremost among them the seizures that had put his son in intensive care. Finally, the gravity of the situation struck him, and he shifted his focus to the dire condition of his child.

For two days, the Moore's newborn was in a deep coma and on the third he passed away. The devastation that Dennis and his wife experienced was incalculable. Days passed as the two tried to deal with their horrible tragedy, and then Mrs. Moore noticed her husband sitting on the patio staring up at the sky. His expression was a portrait of serenity.

"What are you looking at?" she inquired.

"It's *back*," he muttered.

129

"What are you talking about? What's back, Dennis?"

After hesitating, he confessed that the cloud he had seen his entire life had returned.

"Huh … *where?*"

"Directly above, but you won't see it. Nobody ever has."

Amanda shielded her eyes from the sun as she peered upward. Suddenly she let out a squeal. "I see it. Oh my *God!* I see it and …"

Wide smiles covered their faces and tears began flowing from their eyes. The cloud had, indeed, returned, and this time it was different from what it had ever been. In the center of the tiny cumulus was the face of their late son.

#

Body Park

Nearly all the best people are dead!
— Punch

"Hey, I ate a freaking jar of Pickled Snake Head Fish washed down by African Pee Cola, so you can do this," declared Howie Clarkson.

"Yeah, it's a piece of cake compared to what you jerks had me do. Run naked through Wal-Mart, man," added Bill Carter.

"Me, too. Bungee jumping with my fear of heights," recalled Sim Fowler. "All you have to do is survive some flesh-eating zombies."

It was Irv McKenna's turn to take on the challenge devised by his so-called buddies. He was the last of the four to face the music, and he felt more than ready to demonstrate his mettle. Whether it would end the ill-conceived tradition was another matter. The schemes they imposed on one another were beyond weird, but they had certainly enlivened things. No one complained of being bored anymore.

"Bullshit. Dead is *dead*. I don't know why people make such a big thing about dead people. They were just like us when they were alive. Now, everybody thinks of them as creepy monsters. It's kind of sad, you know," replied Irv, responding to the cajoling over what he had to do.

"Hey, rotting corpses are pretty damn creepy, my friend," countered Clarkson.

Spending the night at the Doane Cadaver Farm was his brainchild. It was something he knew he could never attempt, so it struck him as a perfect dare for Irv.

"I'm more concerned about being arrested for trespassing than anything else," protested Irv.

"No one's going to call the cops. They're all dead," chuckled Fowler.

"Don't worry. If you survive the night, we'll spring for your bail if you get busted," goaded Sim.

"With friends like you ..." said Irv, emptying his beer glass.

"Better bring a supply of Depends tomorrow night," said Fowler, now laughing full out.

∗ ∗ ∗

The group waited until close to midnight to deposit Irv at the corpse compound. They brought along a stepladder to help him over the ivy covered brick wall.

"Have a peaceful night, Irvy boy," said Fowler, retracting the ladder as Irv sat at the top of the rampart.

"Quiet as a graveyard. You should sleep the sleep of the dead tonight," joshed Bill.

"I'll come back when I drop off these guys, so if you chicken out, just shout ... or scream like a little girl. I'll be parked right here," snickered Howie.

"Yeah, yeah ... get lost, you jerks. I've got to get my beauty rest," answered Irv, disappearing over the wall.

As soon as he landed on the other side, he cast the beam of his flashlight across the area before him. *Looks like a park*, he thought, and then he saw a body. At first he recoiled at the sight of the bloated corpse. *A woman ... it's a woman*, he surmised, moving a couple steps in its direction. *Young, too ... maybe thirty.*

Irv moved the narrow shaft of his flashlight along the ground to the right of the dead female. Not twenty feet away was a fully clothed corpse propped against a tree. Most of its face had decomposed, creating a grotesquely sardonic grin.

"Now aren't you the handsome one?" muttered Irv, attempting to defuse a growing sense of apprehension. *Come on, Irv. They're harmless ... just poor dead folks. Remember?* he told himself, moving his flashlight away from the seated figure.

Irv's eyes had fully adjusted to the darkness and the full moon no longer necessitated the use of his Eveready. The landscape was well illuminated, revealing more occupants of the corpse farm. In a nearby tree, a body hung from a limb like a laundry bag. Its skeletal arms moved slightly when the wind picked up for a moment. A shoe covered one foot and a sock the other. Denim overalls contained the desiccated remains of the farms' tenant.

At the base of the tall oak, Irv spotted another stiff, this one partially covered by a blanket of leaves. He could not determine its gender but figured it was likely female because of the length of its frizzy hair. Like the visage of the body against the adjacent tree, the face of the prone cadaver was disfigured. Its blank eyes were open, and they bulged from their hollow sockets, like an Alien Invader Zim Girl doll.

Okay, let's just snuggle up here and join our slumbering friends in dreamland. Make the night go faster. Irv nestled into the soft mound unaware that a leathery hand protruded from it. Although what he had seen had unnerved him, Irv felt exhausted. But, given the circumstances, it took a while for him to fall asleep. When he finally did, it was deep.

*   *   *

We have an intruder in our midst, said a voice rising from the naked female body. **Who is it? It's alive.**

I see it, responded the tree corpse. **Disgusting. It has a heartbeat. Not one of the staff. A stranger.**

Why is it here? No civilians ever come here, observed the half covered cadaver. **Wish we could do something about him. He has no right violating the sanctity of the farm.**

This is so humiliating. Look at me, all bloated and decomposing, moaned the unclothed woman. *This is what he sees. Not the beauty I was. I didn't bargain for this when I signed to have my body placed here. I didn't think I'd be gawked at by some damn outsider. I was only thirty-three when I died of a dumb brain aneurism. I was a model.*

We've heard that before, Keri. We all know you were lovely, so give it a rest, if you know what I mean, bristled the sitting corpse.

Don't let it bother you. The mortal doesn't know who you were, sweetie, said the hanging body.

Why did they put me out here without my clothes? I've lost any dignity. This is the worst thing that ever happened to me.

Worse than dying? inquired the recumbent carcass.

Absolutely! I wish I were alive. I'd be able to do something. This is a complete nightmare. If only leaves would conceal me like they have some of you.

*　　　*　　　*

A tormented wail undetected by breathing beings continued until dawn, despite the pleading of the deceased woman's cohorts to stop. Meanwhile, a noise heard by most living humans drew Irv from his solid slumber. *The guys*, thought Irv, responding to the car horn. As he rubbed the sleep from his eyes, he took in his surroundings in the morning light. *Nice place, but I wouldn't want to die here*, he snickered. *Why did they let their bodies be put here? Why would they agree to such a thing? Embarrassing. Jeez, just bury or burn me.*

Irv's attention was suddenly drawn to the naked and bloated body of the female. *Poor thing. Bet you were a beauty once. Look at you. Porcelain skin ... okay, maybe a few cracks.* Irv stood over the body while a feeling of sadness came over him. He removed his jacket and covered the dead woman.

As he did so, he thought he detected a slight change in her expression. When he looked again, he saw that there had been no change. *Whoa, better get out of here before you lose it.*

With some effort, Irv managed to climb to the top of the wall. His friends were standing on the other side.

"We thought the living-dead had ripped you apart and eaten your organs," said Howie, holding the stepladder as Irv descended it.

"Get real. There's just a bunch of harmless bodies in there," grumbled Irv.

"You mean a bunch of disgusting, decaying corpses," added Sim.

"Hey," barked Irv, "they're *people*, too!"

#

Pick Your Poison

And the Devil did grin, for his darling sin
Is pride that apes humility.

— Coleridge

Something distracted Cecil Winthrop from the road ahead. It felt like the weight of a boulder and caused him to veer his new Audi Q5 hybrid into a telephone pole. While the collision was not exceptional in terms of damage to the car, it proved sadly fatal for its driver. Thus Cecil had not lived to receive what he had regarded as the ultimate recognition for his extraordinary career—an honorary degree from his alma mater. The accident occurred only two miles from the campus of Dultry College, where the ceremonies were to take place. He had been alone on his way to the institution because he was eager to meet up with his former classmates for an early brunch at The Rat. His wife and daughter planned to join up with him before the commencement exercises got underway at noon.

Cecil's childhood had all the earmarks of a 1940s B-movie melodrama. His life had begun in poverty in a western Pennsylvania mining community. His mother had cleaned houses while his father labored as a roof bolter in the underground shafts of the Cleary Coal Company. On two occasions, Perry Winthrop had suffered on-the-job injuries, resulting in long periods of convalescence. His relationship with his four sons was not a cordial one, as the elder Winthrop had long been afflicted by serious bouts of melancholy. For him, the world was as drab and cheerless as the mines in which he toiled for low wages.

By the time Cecil was in grade school he was certain he wanted a very different life from that of his parents. Neither had graduated from high school, and so it became his first major life goal to get his diploma. This pleased his mother who preached the gospel of education to her offspring.

"If you don't finish school, you won't get anywhere in this world. I missed out and look what I'm doing, cleaning up other people's messes," declared Mrs. Winthrop countless times.

While Cecil took her words to heart, his older brothers saw little value in pursuing useless studies when they could make real money in the mines. Despite their mother's pleading for them to remain in school, one by one they quit when they reached the age of sixteen. So it was one of Mrs. Winthrop's proudest and happiest days when her youngest child donned a cap and gown and gave his high school's valedictory address.

*   *   *

Four years later, Cecil's mother would see that same ambitious son graduate with highest honors from the state university. By then his father had died, and the oldest of his three brothers had taken his mother in. Cecil promised himself that as soon as he was financially able, he would give his mother a better life. And he was able to do this sooner than expected as he quickly rose in the ranks of the company where he worked as an account representative. Little more than three years out of college, he was promoted to sales manager. A nice salary jump came with the advancement, and Cecil found his mother a small apartment of her own and paid the monthly rent. Doing this filled him with great satisfaction and pride, although it inspired a degree of jealousy in his blue-collar siblings. They appreciated his generosity but felt Cecil had become smug about his success and critical about their modest way of life. From their perspective, he was becoming like the people who ran the mines—haute and imperious. The Cleary family clearly looked down on their low-level employees.

"Now don't get too good for us, Ce Ce," counseled Ben Winthrop.

While Cecil laughed off his brother's remark, deep down he did feel superior to his siblings. He had achieved something they never would. If that made him appear superior, so be it, he thought. *I can't help what I am, and what I am is pretty damn impressive.*

He continued to rise in the business world, and before he reached thirty, he became vice president in his company. Two years later, he was lured to a larger business and given the title of chief operating officer. It was there that he met his wife, Tara. So as not to give the impression of preferential treatment by her spouse, she left the firm after they were married. During the years that followed, she would give birth to a son and daughter. Unlike what he'd experienced as a child, Cecil made certain his children had every possible opportunity, which included private schools and frequent travel. Life was better than he'd ever imagined, but he was determined to rise even further. His drive to accumulate more wealth and the reputation that went with it was far from sated.

*   *   *

By the time his children entered high school, he had risen to president of his company, and his wife had joined several civic groups. As his close partner in the quest to reach as far as he could in his career and life, Tara urged him to become involved in charity work. Soon his effort on behalf of the community brought him accolades and awards. It even inspired talk of his entering politics. Cecil was intensely pleased with everything he had accomplished and was deeply gratified by the formidable respect shown him by everyone.

I've got it all, he'd remind himself with ever-increasing frequency thrilled by a life that had turned out the way he dreamed it would. And things got even better as his children graduated with distinction from ivy-league colleges and his wife assumed the leadership role in the local gardening club and women's auxiliary group. The Winthrops exemplified the phrase "pillars of the community." Then came the honorary doctorate. Cecil excitedly invited everyone he knew to a lavish dinner to celebrate the honor.

"You'll all have to call me *Dr.* Winthrop from now on," he half-joked at the gathering.

How far I have come, he congratulated himself, as the guests raised their glasses in a toast.

"To the man of the hour!" declared his second in command, Bill Castle. *Man of the* century *you mean*, thought Cecil, bowing to the admiring throng.

It was in this rapturous state of mind that Cecil headed to the rendezvous with his Dultry classmates on the day of his further elevation. As he drove, he suddenly experienced a physical irritation so profound that he lost control of his vehicle and slammed into the utility pole, leaving his glorious world behind.

* * *

His death was a shock to everyone who knew him, and his family was beyond devastated. The coroner's report of the incident that caused Cecil's death reached Tara Winthrop early on the day of her husband's funeral.

"Oh my, God! This is ... terrible. Humiliating. The press can't get this," she cried to her children.

"What's wrong, Mother?"

The report of their father's unfortunate mishap detailed the exact cause of his death. To everyone it had been unclear why a relatively minor accident would kill anyone, especially since the car's airbag had deployed. When the Winthrop children read the coroner's description, they, too, were aghast.

"You see what I mean? That can't appear in the papers. It will stain your father's good memory. He'll be the subject of all kinds of insulting comments, and all he did in his life will be belittled. Everyone will think of him … and *us*, differently. All we've achieved and worked for will be diminished."

"Let's call the newspapers and ask them not to publish that detail," suggested Ronny Winthrop to his mother and sister.

He was informed by both of the town's papers that it was too late to consider his request. Neither would reveal what they had printed, saying that he could soon read the obit himself, since the papers were about to be delivered. The Winthrops held their breath until their newspaper arrived, and then they let out a collective moan after reading Cecil's death notice.

Because of his lofty status in the community, his tragic passing was a front-page story. The headline in one of the papers read:

Prominent businessman and community leader dies from picking his nose.

The story continued:

The autopsy revealed that Cecil L. Wintrop's index finger had been lodged in his nostril upon impact and that it had apparently punctured his brain.

Cecil's eldest brother gave the eulogy at his funeral. The Winthrops' weeping intensified when he spoke, though not because of what he said about his tremendously accomplished sibling. He could not help but chuckle whenever he thought about what led to his esteemed brother's untimely death.

#

When the Mountains Rise

He said, 'I look for butterflies
that sleep among the wheat.'
                — Lewis Carroll

Fourteen-year-old Cameron Perkins imagined huge naval ships sailing through the dense growth at harvest time when the wheat stood higher than he did. In his mind's eye the gently rolling plains resembled the ocean he had seen only in books. When the parched winds blew, the crop would heave and surge, and he could picture the bows of great steel vessels disappearing and reappearing in the turbulent sea of grain.

"You think battleships could cross the fields?" he'd asked his grandfather, Will Perkins, as he busily prepared to cut down the amber waves with his American Harvester.

"When the mountains rise, son. When the mountains rise," came the old man's standard reply to anything he viewed as beyond the realm of possibility.

"I bet they could, grandpa."

"Yeah, and if wishes were horses, beggars would ride, Cam. Now give me a hand here. We've, uh, got to flatten the surf before them warships plough through here."

Cameron loved his grandfather as much as he had his deceased parents and grandmother. The three Perkinses had come to a grisly end in a car accident in 1948, leaving their only child and grandson in the sole care of the family's 71-year-old patriarch. Since then, life revolved around him and his grandfather on the 1200-acre farm. For a long time after the unthinkable tragedy, deep sadness had turned their once happy world into a bleak and sullen place, but gradually the darkness lifted and the pain of their loss lessened. Although things became more bearable, Cameron would sometimes find his grandfather in front of the fireplace mantle talking to the photograph of his departed wife. He never interrupted his grandfather on those occasions or asked him what he said to the woman he had known as Granny Hildy. It seemed like it would violate his grandfather's privacy to do so. Cameron didn't want him to know he had seen him crying, even though he'd been seen weeping over his parents' pictures.

"Well, at least you're not suffering from a drought," said his grandfather, wrapping his arm around Cameron's shoulder. "Maybe you could shed some of them big tears on the crop."

The year of the life-shattering accident had seen the fields turn to dust in one of the worst droughts on record. It had been so bad the annual harvest festival had been cancelled, and the nearest neighbors—some five miles away—had abandoned their farm. Their son, Dwight, was Cameron's age, and the two had become best friends before his parents moved in with their own some distance away. Cameron had never felt so alone during the year that followed. Compounding his sense of isolation was his grandfather's new stoicism. Before the loss of his wife, he had always been quick to add his two cents to any conversation. Now he mostly spoke in monosyllables, which left Cameron thirsting for verbal companionship.

Young Perkins attempted to enliven things by suggesting that they take a trip after the coming harvest, but the old man seemed determined to remain in his melancholy state and rejected the idea out of hand.

"Why'd we do that?"

"I've never been anywhere, grandpa. Can't we go down to Omaha to see the zoo and go to the movies?"

"There are things to do after bringing in the crop. Responsibilities don't end when the cutting does, Cam."

"Okay, then. Can we at least get a TV set? There's nothing to do around here at night."

"Sleep is *what* we do at night. 'Sides, televisions cost a heap and we likely wouldn't get a signal out here anyway."

143

"If we had a high antenna like the Caufields did. They could get a station. I saw it myself. We could build a real tall one … a hundred feet high."

"When the mountains rise, kiddo," responded Mr. Perkins.

The next year passed without any measurable change, except for the weather. The arid soil was revived by an autumn of heavy rain and a winter of deep snow. The resulting bumper crop helped to lift his grandfather's flagging spirits, and his slowly returning cheerfulness enhanced Cameron's mood as well. Despite the upswing in spirits, however, the elder Perkins suffered from a nagging cough and arthritis that made his fingers swell and ache.

"Maybe, after harvest, we'll go visit your Aunt Giselle out in Colorado. She lives in a place called Lyons."

Cameron was excited about the prospect of a trip and he counted the days until the time to reap began. But as it neared, a problem arose that threatened disaster. His grandfather's usual seasonal hires were not available. One had moved away and the other was laid up with a broken leg.

"We can do it ourselves, grandpa," offered Cameron.

"When the mountains rise. No way we can do it without Bo and Jessie. Hard enough with them."

As the time for harvesting the hundreds of acres of wheat arrived, Cameron's grandfather conceded that there was nothing left to do but bring in as much of the crop with the aid of his grandson as was possible. Despite a widespread search, he had not been able to find another person to help with the task.

"Guess we're really on our own now, Cam. Thought things were hopeless without your Pa lending a hand. Now there's no Bo and Jessie. Lord, help us."

Over the next week, the Perkins pair worked from sunrise to sunset gathering and hauling what they could of the bountiful yield. Both Cameron and Will drove tractors with sickle mowers attached. Cameron had driven the farm-only vehicle once before, but after a few hours at the wheel, he felt confident. In fact, cutting through the forest of grain was the best he had felt since losing his friend.

Despite their formidable efforts, however, most of the farm remained blanketed with the uncut crop. At the same time, Cameron's concern for his grandfather's health rose. At the end of the day, Will was totally spent and had no appetite. He would drop into his recliner and fall asleep almost immediately, awaking every so often from a fit of coughing. During one of his grandfather's spasms, Cameron noticed blood on his handkerchief. At the sight of it, his apprehension soared.

"Grandpa, you need a doctor. We should go to the hospital," he pleaded.

"When the mountains rise, Cam. We got work to do," replied his grandfather, closing his eyes and breathing heavily.

The next morning the elder Perkins appeared pale and acted listless. He sipped his coffee but pushed aside the eggs Cameron had scrambled.

"You need to eat for your strength, grandpa. Can't work like you are."

"Not going to work. We're going to my sister's. You can stay with her awhile. I'll come back and finish this up."

"You can't do it alone! You're sick," protested Cameron.

"I'll be fine. You'll have a better time with your aunt. She's a good woman. You'll like her. I'll fetch you in about a month. I wrote down her address. You should keep it on you in case ..."

"But ..."

"Now, no argument, please. Get your things together and we'll hit the road. You're a good boy, Cam, and you've been a big help. But some things need more help than you can give them, and this is one of those times. Besides, we got enough cut to survive 'til the next one. That's what counts."

Cameron reluctantly packed his things and placed them in the back of the pickup truck.

"Please let me stay here and help with the harvest," implored Cameron again, as he took the seat next to his grandfather.

Without responding, Will Perkins put the truck in gear and drove down the dirt driveway leading to another unpaved road. In ten minutes they reached the single lane paved road that would take them to the two-lane blacktop that ran west.

"Should get there tomorrow if this old heap holds up," offered Will, trying to suppress another coughing spell.

By mid-afternoon they had reached North Platte, and Will had reluctantly ceded to Cameron's request to visit Buffalo Bill's homestead.

"Thanks, Grandpa. The sign says it isn't far."

"Far enough, but what the heck. I'm curious, too. My Pa, your great granddad, actually knew him."

"Really? Did he kill all those Indians they say he did?"

"No, I think he just hired them for his Wild West show."

Cameron and his grandfather spent the night in a small cabin in Ogallala, a town not far from the northeastern corner of Colorado. In the morning, it took him a considerable effort to raise his grandfather from sleep. When he succeeded, he was frightened by the look of confusion on his face. Several seconds passed before Will said anything, and when he did, Cameron's fear increased.

"We got more wheat to cut down on the west third. Let's get going. It won't harvest by itself," mumbled Will, lifting himself up with his elbows.

"Grandpa. We're on our way to Aunt Giselle's house. Don't you remember?"

After a few moments, Will Perkin's eyes gathered focus. "Sure, I do. Just was dreaming is all. Better get going, huh?"

Cameron was encouraged by his grandfather's suddenly renewed interest in breakfast. After consuming a meal that included eggs and flapjacks, the duo climbed into the dust-covered pickup and continued their westward trek.

For the first time during their journey, they engaged in lively conversation that included fond recollections of their beloved lost family members.

"Your Granny Hildy was the sweetest gal I ever met, not that I met many ladies. Only a dozen in my high school class, but Hildegard was the prettiest of the lot, I can promise you that," recalled Will.

"You think people who die ever come back to visit us so we can see them again?" asked Cameron, looking at his grandfather's angular profile that had always reminded him of Abe Lincoln.

"When the mountains rise, but not in this world, I'm afraid." His grandfather sighed as they crossed the state line into Colorado. "Well, here we are. Your first state outside of Nebraska, boy. Congratulations! You're a man of the world now."

Cameron was thrilled to have finally gone beyond the border of his home state. It was something he had long awaited, but he was disappointed that there was no dramatic change in the landscape.

"I thought it would look different, grandpa."

"Oh, it will soon. Don't you fret. It will look unlike anything you've ever seen."

"When?"

"In a couple hours. Don't be ..."

Will made a loud gasp and his body stiffened. The truck began to leave the road, and Cameron grabbed the steering wheel and directed the vehicle onto the dirt shoulder, pressing the break as hard as he could.

"Grandpa! Grandpa! What's the matter?" screamed Cameron, but he got no response.

Will's face was ashen and beginning to turn blue. Small bubbles oozed from his lips. *He's having a heart attack. Get help before he dies*, thought Cameron, jumping from the truck. But there were no cars to flag down. *What can I do! He's dying ... he's dying!* Several minutes passed without a sign of another vehicle. Sobbing, Cameron went around to the driver's side and pushed his grandfather away from the steering wheel. *I got to get help. Find a hospital. There's nothing here.*

Cameron moved the truck back onto the road and pressed the accelerator to the floor, causing the vehicle to jerk violently. He had never handled a standard shift before. The tractor he had driven had only forward and backward gears. After several attempts, he managed to get the truck into a higher gear that gave him cruising speed. By the time he had come to a town, he knew his grandfather was no longer alive, and he had decided to take him to his sister's house rather than someplace unfamiliar along the way.

Cameron tried without success to stem the tide of tears that rolled down his cheeks as he drove on. *Grandpa ... poor Grandpa*, he moaned, feeling like the last person on the planet. And then, very slowly, the foothills of the Rocky Mountains began to appear on the horizon. Soon he could make out the real mountains farther west. The sight lifted his spirits slightly, and the closer he got to the snow-capped peaks, the less hopelessness he felt.

"Look, Grandpa. The mountains *are* rising. I bet you can see Granny Hildy now ... and Mom and Dad, too."

#

Purple Hearts

In love there is peculiar magic.
— Lord Byron

Barry Reardon was a short timer. In fourteen days he would be shipped home from Afghanistan and reunited with his wife of just two years. He had never looked forward to anything so much in his life. As he put on his combat gear for his team's daily IED sweep in Now Zad, he placed an X over the current date on the calendar hanging from his locker.

"Two weeks!" he shouted to his fellow soldiers. "Won't have to look at you dogfaces any more."

"Yeah, if you don't get your ass blown off by the towel heads," responded Sergeant Neil, his squad leader.

"No way. I got a beautiful lady waiting for me, so not gonna let any Tally-Ban get my butt before she does."

"Okay, you grunts, let's head out," ordered Billings.

Less than an hour into the patrol, Reardon stepped on a land mine and died instantly.

When the Casualty Notification Officers rang Linda Reardon's doorbell in Roanoke, Virginia, she was buttering her English muffin.

"Coming!" she shouted, throwing on her robe.

The two uniformed men at the door caught her off guard momentarily, but then the reality of the situation became all too evident.

"Oh my God!!" she wailed, leaning against the doorframe.

Linda did not have to hear the soldier's words to know that what she feared most had happened.

*   *   *

A month after her husband's funeral, Linda's deep grief had been partially replaced by anger over the violent manner in which her loved one had perished. *So young ... just starting out. We were just starting out.* She had returned to work but still could not join any social gatherings without feeling a wrenching absence for the first and only man she had ever loved. A tribute at the local Marine base honoring her fallen husband was the first time she readily agreed to be with a group since his funeral. It was the one public occasion she would not miss. She had also promised Barry's parents that she would represent them at the event. They did not have the financial wherewithal to return to California from Ohio to witness their son being awarded the Purple Heart posthumously.

The day of the event, Linda pulled herself together and arrived at the base minutes before the medal presentation was scheduled to get underway. She had been told to bring a brief message for her deceased husband, as it was a tradition to attach one to a heart-shaped purple balloon for launching at the conclusion of the tribute. She had thought long and hard about what to say, but in the end all she could write was, "I will love you forever, darling. Linda." She placed the small slip of paper from her memo pad into her purse, but took it out several times to look at it. Each time she read the message her throat tightened and she fought back tears. *You're such a wreck. You'll never get through this.* When she noticed her address on the note, she considered rewriting it on a blank piece of paper. *What does it matter?* she told herself, glancing at her watch. *Late ... damn it!*

An officer greeted Linda at the base's entrance and escorted her to a small landscaped common in which stood a small platform with a lectern and two chairs. A contingent of Marines in their dress blues comprised the whole audience. Linda had resisted the idea of inviting friends and coworkers to the event, because she expected to be too emotionally distraught to deal with them.

"I'm sorry for your loss, Mrs. Reardon. I hope this recognition of your husband's courage and dedication gives you some peace," said the officer, pointing her to a seat on the stage.

He then tapped on the microphone to see if it was working and proceeded to speak.

"There is a verse in the Bible which reads: 'Greater love has no one than this, that he lay down his life for his friends.' On that same note, the brave men and women who have made the ultimate sacrifice to preserve liberty for all Americans must never be forgotten ..."

The soldiers in attendance stood at parade rest during the officer's short speech, and when he presented Linda with the box containing the Purple Heart, they snapped to attention and saluted.

"On behalf of the country and the United States Marines, we thank you and your family for your patriotism, commitment, and sacrifice."

Linda stared at the ribbon and felt an instant and profound connection with it. *My brave, dear husband,* she thought on the verge of sobbing. She closed the case and held it to her chest.

"Mrs. Reardon, your message?" asked the presiding officer, reaching in back of the platform where a helium balloon had been tied.

Linda was surprised that she had not noticed it until the officer held it before her.

"Oh, yes, I'm sorry."

She removed the note from her purse and handed it to the officer, who tied it to the balloon's string. He then handed it to her.

"Please release it when you feel you want to."

Thoughts of her husband rushed through her mind as she held the balloon. She could feel it pull upward. *Is it you, Barry? I am with you always,* she whispered and let it go. The balloon soon drifted out of sight, eventually deflating and landing two miles away in a yard not far from Linda's house.

That night she placed her husband's Purple Heart on the pillow next to hers. For the first time since she'd been informed of his death, Linda was able to sleep as deeply as she had when Barry was in bed with her.

∗   ∗   ∗

The urge to do harm again was consuming Liam Poem. It had been almost six months since he had tortured and killed, and he longed for the thrill and satisfaction it gave him. His victims were all women, mostly young, and thus far there had been three of them. He hungered for a fourth, and the message attached to the withered balloon he'd found on his lawn seemed like a gift from the gods— signed, sealed, and delivered. *Who was this Linda, Was she pretty ...* young? he wondered. He would find out. The address on the note revealed that she lived nearby.

The next morning, Liam drove to 21 Chesterton Street and parked. He waited patiently as a predator does its unsuspecting prey. Eventually, his persistence paid off. *She is pretty ... and young,* reveled Liam, watching Linda as she placed a trash barrel at the curb. *Yummy, you're going to be so much fun.* After he saw her, he began planning how he would draw her into his web. *Wait in the bushes next to her door after dark. She has to come out eventually. When she does, grab her and put her out with the ether, like you've done before. It will work again.*

Liam decided to initiate his attack sooner than later. He usually took his time before he launched into action, but his desire to sate his appetite for violence had become more urgent since seeing Linda. To him she was by far the most attractive of the women he had raped and murdered, and his fantasies about doing the same to her filled every moment of his waking hours as well as his dreams. He would not take her life as quickly as he had the others. He would savor every act of penetration, every cut of her flesh with his surgical instruments. He would rejoice in her every cry for mercy.

Just as the fates had delivered the name and address of Liam's next victim, they had also accommodated him by quickly availing him of his object of desire. Linda had decided to make a quick trip to the local variety store to pick up a few necessities. Two steps outside of her door, she felt someone grab her and cover her face with a cloth. When she regained consciousness, she found herself bound and blindfolded. She tried to scream but the gag in her mouth prevented anything beyond a muffled shriek.

Liam was sitting not three feet in front of Linda with his genitals exposed. Every sound and move his prisoner made aroused him further.

"Hello, Linda. We're going to have a little party," he said, removing the gag from her mouth.

"Who are you? What are you doing? Untie me!"

"No, I don't think that's possible. But I will remove your clothes so we can get really friendly."

"Don't touch me. My husband ..."

"Will do what? He's dead, isn't he ... your little war hero? You think he'll mind if I have some naughty fun with you? No I doubt he will, given where he is."

"Please let me go. Why are you doing this to me?"

"Because I need to. It won't be too bad ... at first. We'll start off slowly and then get more serious as we go along."

Liam reached for the hem of her skirt and began raising it.

"Such sweet legs. Bet they lead to something even sweeter."

Linda attempted to squirm, but she was firmly anchored to the cold surface she'd been placed on. As her assailant's hand began to drift up the inside of her thigh, she heard a loud grunt followed by a resounding crash. Immediately after it, she discovered that her body was no longer shackled.

"What … *who's* there?"

Though it was deadly still, Linda felt she could sense a familiar presence. With trepidation, she removed the blindfold. The room was dimly lit, but she could discern a man's body heaped against the wall. She surveyed her surroundings, fearing that at any moment someone or something would leap out of the shadows at her. Then she saw stairs leading up from what was apparently a basement. She made her way to them and climbed to the top, her legs feeling like they might give out at any moment. The door to the basement was slightly ajar, and she carefully peeked out. A hallway led to a front door, and Linda decided to make a run for it despite her trembling limbs.

I made it … I'm okay, she thought, as she reached outside.

"Help! *Please* … help me!" she cried out.

A woman across the street from where Linda had finally collapsed began running to her aid. As the responder approached, Linda noticed that she had been clutching an object in her right hand. When she opened it, she let out a gasp of recognition.

"*Barry* … *Barry*," she murmured, staring at his Purple Heart and then clutching it to *her* heart.

#

If a Tree Falls in the Forest ...

Nothing ever becomes real till it is experienced.
— John Keats

The last thing Brandon was about to do was point out the obvious to his fellow commuters. If other drivers didn't see the glimmering obelisk that towered above the highway at Exit 11, it was their loss. *How could they not see this incredible object?* he wondered. *Why am I the only one looking at it?* Its ever-changing colors were more than awe inspiring to him. They were captivating to the point that on a couple of occasions he had almost driven off the road staring at the unique vision.

Finally, one day at work it got to him that nobody had even mentioned the existence of the breath-taking sight. Not a single soul claimed to have seen it, even though many of his cohorts took the exact same route to work as he did.

"Come on!" he exclaimed, frustrated. "You can't miss it. It's incredible! Reaches to the sky ... for heaven's sake!"

"Where is this thing again?" asked his cubical mate.

"At Exit 11. You were in front of me this morning getting off the highway at *that* exit, Gil, and you're saying you didn't see it? I saw *it*, and I saw *you*."

"I guess not. I'll look for it on the way home."

"Can't fathom how you overlooked it. It's tall as a skyscraper and changes ... first blue, then red, then green, then something else. Some shades I've never even seen before. Can't even describe them. "

*   *   *

The next morning Brandon was eager to get his fellow workers' impressions of the Protean column, but to his astonishment, once again no one seemed to have seen it.

155

"You guys are just pulling my leg, and it's not funny either," protested Brandon. "What's wrong with you people?"

His fellow telemarketers just shook their heads in confusion and went back to work. *Idiots!* thought Brandon. *Obviously, they're blind. Well, too bad for them.*

On his way to the office the next day, Brandon became so entranced by the morphing obelisk that he lost control of his car and drove right into it. For a moment everything went black . . . and then he heard a man's voice.

"Sir, are you all right?"

A state police officer peered at Brandon through his driver's side window.

"Yes ... yes, I'm fine, officer. I can't believe I'm not dead after hitting that tower.

"*Tower*, sir?"

"The one changing colors right back ..."

The lawman opened the car door and took hold of Brandon's arm.

"Sir, please step out of the car and breathe into this device."

\#

Contrails

Miles and miles distant though the last line be ...
— Dante Rossetti

Before Billy Wyler's eyes had even opened for the first time, some part of his infant brain registered vivid white lines crossing the primordial darkness behind his closed lids. By the time he was four years old, similar streaks in the infinite western Nebraska sky drew his attention.

"Mommy, what are those?" asked Billy, pointing upward.

"Those are jet fumes," replied Marion Wyler.

"Well, not exactly," corrected his Uncle Frank. "Those are trails of condensed water from aircraft ... jets. They're called contrails."

"I stand corrected," said Marion, poking her brother-in-law in the arm.

"Contails?" repeated Billy.

"No, con*trails*. There's an 'r' in the word."

"Con*tails*," blurted Billy.

"Close enough, little man. Now I'd best be getting home."

"Thanks for fixing the bathroom tank, Frank. Really appreciate it. Wouldn't know what to do without you."

"Well, maybe Kevin will get out soon and ..."

Marion's expression darkened, and Frank dropped the subject. Her husband had been confined to the state mental facility for two years and the prospect of his being released anytime in the near future was remote as far as she was concerned. In all honesty, she felt unprepared to deal with his return, especially if any of the behavioral issues that had caused him to be committed still existed. His manic delusions about extraterrestrials and consequent camping out on the roof naked while awaiting their arrival had been the last straw.

"See you guys day after tomorrow for the cutting," said Frank, heading to his pickup.

Billy remained on the front porch staring at the sky as his mother disappeared inside the house. When she returned a half-hour later, her son's gaze was still fixed on the heavens.

"Well, you sure like to look at the planes, huh? They go far off and none of them land nearby. No one's coming here on one of those big jets. Maybe Denver, but I think if a plane is really high up in the sky, it's probably going much further. Like that one there," said Marion, pointing to a glimmering silver speck in the firmament. "It could be going to San Francisco, even Hawaii."

Billy's intense interest in the passing aircraft began to concern Marion. Day after day she would find him looking upward as if hypnotized. The vacant expression on his face added to her anxiety.

"Honey, what are you looking at? There are just some white lines ... contrails, like your Uncle Frank said. Can't be all that exciting. Come on. Go collect some eggs. Besides, looking up at the sun will injure your eyes."

"They're funny," mumbled Billy.

"What's funny?"

"The con*tails*."

"Why?" asked Marion, feeling unsettled.

The fear that he might be following in his father's footsteps began to enter her thoughts.

"'Cause," answered Billy, skipping off to the hen house.

*   *   *

What was capturing Billy's interest were the words, even phrases, and short sentences he saw forming in the vapor trails left by the passing aircraft. Indeed, his vocabulary was advanced for his age. His mother had read to him nightly, insisting that her son learn basic written language in advance of his attending school. Billy now believed the sky was communicating with him, and he was delighted with the very idea.

"Happy boy," he said to his mother as she found him sitting on the porch steps.

"Yes, you are a happy boy," she repeated, sitting down next to him.

Billy pointed to the sky. "Good boy."

"Yes, a very good boy," said Marion, looking into her child's eyes.

"Play with the bunnies," Billy mumbled.

"Do you see something up there, honey?" inquired Marion.

"Going to play with the bunnies," he said, disregarding his mother's question.

What is going on with him? Marion wondered, feeling as if some invisible force was directing the actions of her son. *Oh, God, please, no. Not like his father.*

Kevin Wyler had behaved similarly on several occasions. Marion had encountered him talking to something unseen when he was in the wheat field and in the livestock pen behind the barn. This was in the early stage of what hadn't been recognized as his breakdown. In the months that followed, things got decidedly worse. Kevin had begun to insist that he was communicating with beings from another galaxy. He claimed they had chosen him to come visit their planet, and they would soon take him there.

Billy had not seen his father in two years and by now had mostly forgotten what he looked like. Marion had resisted taking her son to visit him in the institution, because he continued to behave bizarrely. Kevin's brother, Frank, had mixed feelings about keeping the boy from his own father but kept his views on the subject to himself, sparing Marion further stress.

*   *   *

Two hours had passed since Marion had seen Billy. He had failed to respond to her calls, so she went to look for him in the barn where the rabbits were kept.

"There you are. Didn't you hear …?"

Next to her son lay a dead rabbit that had apparently been crushed by the rock next to its bloodied body.

"What … *what* happened, Billy?"

Her son slowly turned to her and the look in his eyes caused her to gasp. They appeared detached from his being … alien.

"Oh, God, Billy. What happened? Did you do this?"

His body was rigid and cold to the touch as she put her arms around him.

"It said to," Billy muttered.

"Huh? What said to?"

"The contails."

"What are you saying, sweetie?"

"It said 'kill the bunny.'"

"Oh, baby … what's the matter with you?" whimpered Marion, lifting Billy, and running from the barn.

"Look, mommy. See … *kill bunny*," said Billy, pointing upward.

Two sleek contrails crisscrossed the cloudless sky. They reminded Marion of a crucifix, and the thought made her shiver.

*   *   *

"Kids do crazy things, sometimes damn mean things cause they don't know better," replied Frank when Marion told him about the rabbit incident.

"I hope that's all there is to it."

"What else could it be? Don't worry. I'm sure he knows he did something bad."

Frank had arrived to begin harvesting the small field of wheat he had planted on his sister-in-law's property. In return for his handyman help, Marion had allowed him to cultivate five acres of her farm for his benefit. They both thought it was a perfect exchange.

"Thanks for everything, Frank," said Marion. "It's been tough with Kevin gone."

"I know it has, but thank you for letting me seed the field. How about Billy riding with me in the tractor?"

"He'd like that. I'll go get him."

Marion found her son in his room peering out the window at the sky.

"Uncle Frank wants you to ride with him in the John Deere while he cuts the wheat. That'll be fun, huh?"

Billy did not respond, so Marion tapped him on his shoulder to break his reverie. After a second he turned and looked at his mother, expressionless.

"Are you okay, honey? Why do you keep looking at the sky? There's nothing out there."

"Yes there is," responded Billy, moving past her toward the door.

"Wait ... what do you see?"

Billy let out a giggle. "Things ... words."

Marion looked out of the window at the blank sky.

"I don't see anything. Are you pretending?"

Billy shook his head and ran from the room. Marion returned her gaze out of the window and suddenly felt the weight of the world descend on her. *Oh God*, she moaned, watching her son being lifted into the tractor by his uncle.

"You okay, kiddo?" asked Frank, as he started the motor.

After a long pause, Billy turned to his uncle. "No," he said, smiling, and turned away.

"What's the matter, son?"

"Look," said Billy, pointing to the sky with sudden enthusiasm. "Con*tails*."

*   *   *

Several years passed and Billy exhibited no further fixation on the vapor trails of passing aircraft. After the rabbit event, he'd stopped staring trancelike at the sky. As time passed, Marion began to think of it as an aberration of childhood, and she was profoundly relieved. Although her husband remained institutionalized, her life had settled into an easy rhythm and she had attained a level of contentment she thought would never come. Everything seemed right ... and then it quickly didn't.

A week after Billy graduated from high school, Marion found him staring at the sky and mumbling to himself in the back yard. Her heart sank. *Not again*, she thought. *Please, not again.* She decided not to confront him, hoping it would be an isolated episode, but over the next few days, the scene repeated itself. When she finally asked Billy what he was doing, he giggled as he had fourteen years earlier following the same question.

When her brother-in-law showed up to repair a torn window screen, she informed him of Billy's odd behavior. This time he was not as certain that his nephew's actions were as benign as they had been when he was little.

"Might have him see someone."

"A psychiatrist?"

"Someone who knows about mental stuff. Maybe Kevin's old therapist. What was his name? Dr. Berry?"

"Yes, it was, but he retired a couple of years ago. Do you think Billy really needs a shrink? I don't know what I'll do if he has what his father does."

"Hey, don't even go there. It's probably some little tick that can be handled with some meds. He seems fine otherwise, right?"

"I guess, but when he starts jabbering to the sky, he reminds me of Kevin."

"Find someone he can talk to. Things will be okay. Don't think the worst."

Marion made an appointment with a therapist in Scottsbluff and was relieved when her son did not object to going.

"I don't know why, but if it makes you happy, I'll talk with the guy. I want to get a pair of binoculars at the Sports Mart there anyway."

"What for?"

"So I can see things better. You know," replied Billy nodding skyward.

Marion smiled at her son while fighting back tears.

*   *   *

The messages that Billy saw in the contrails captivated him, especially the ones about things that wanted to harm him and his mother. Animals posed the biggest threat to their wellbeing and now the streaks were warning him about the dangers that his uncle posed—UNCLE FRANK WANTS TO HURT YOU. It upset him that his beloved uncle was a threat to him and his mother, and he resisted the directives from the contrails. Instead, he thought getting rid of the chickens and hog would avert any further contretemps.

When Billy knew his mother was in bed for the evening, he went to the barn and slaughtered the hazardous animals. When the dawn arrived, he was pleased that the message in the sole contrail he could see commended his actions. However, not long after, a new contrail reminded him that his uncle had to be dealt with next.

Not Uncle Frank, please! Billy pleaded, but the vapor trail insisted.

KILL UNCLE … KILL UNCLE! it commanded in huge letters from twenty thousand feet in the air.

Marion was horrified when she discovered the carnage in the barn and knew that it was the act of her son. She immediately called her brother-in-law, who agreed to come right over. She then confronted her son.

"They were going to hurt us," he replied.

"The chickens and hog? Where did you get that crazy notion, Billy? What made you do it, for God's sake?" Billy's eyes moved upward. "Those things … those white lines?"

Billy nodded and smiled.

"They were going to hurt us, and Uncle Frank will, too."

"Uncle Frank?" shouted Marion, her body shaking.

A cloud of dust appeared in the distance.

"It's him," muttered Billy, who then ran into the barn.

In a couple of minutes, Frank pulled up and was greeted by his frantic sister-in-law.

"Thanks for coming. He's in the barn. Said the animals were going to harm us. He said you were going to also."

"I'll talk to him. Let's get him to the hospital."

"Okay," replied Marion, following her brother-in-law to the barn.

"Hang back, Marion. Let me have words with him alone."

Marion watched nervously as Frank disappeared inside. Almost immediately, there was a scream, and her brother-in-law came stumbling out with a pitchfork in his thigh, blood spurting from it.

"Get the sheriff," he yelled, falling to the ground.

After she called for help, Marion ran back to Frank to help staunch the bleeding, but it was too late. The blow had struck an artery and he had quickly bled it out.

The deputy sheriff found Marion in shock next to her brother-in-law's body. The lawman located Billy in a field a couple hundred yards away as he stood motionless with his head upturned.

*   *   *

Billy was committed to the state's facility for the criminally insane. After assaulting two of his fellow inmates, he was placed in an insolated, windowless cell. Guards checked on him at designated intervals. When they did, they invariably found him curled up in a corner mumbling and giggling to himself with his eyes closed tightly. In the darkness of his inner world, contrails formed a thousand different words.

\#

Existential Raccoons

Being is. Being is in-itself. Being is what it is.
—Jean-Paul Sartre

Hillsboro, Minnesota, had a problem—suicidal raccoons. At least that's what Herbert Ramsey believed, and he made his theory known at the emergency town meeting inspired by the recent rash of roadkill.

"Seen 'em just jump in front of cars. They'd be standing on the side of the road, and when a car showed up, they'd draw in their little back legs and spring into the road. Craziest darn thing I ever saw. They were just set on killing themselves. Saw four do it this morning."

"Now how is *that* possible, Herb? Raccoons don't form suicide pacts," observed Town Councilman Ryan Frosby."

"Well, how do you explain over a hundred dead in the last two days?"

"So you think they held a meeting and decided to kill themselves? Why would that be, Herb?"

"I wasn't at their meeting," sneered Herb, "so I can't answer that question, but it sure seems likely they were in league with each other. Had a plan. I mean, a hundred in two days ... c'mon?"

Macy Wilmart, assistant principal of Hillsboro Junior High School, offered another theory.

"Maybe they were driven to it by toxins. Ten Mile River is full of waste from the rubber recycling plant. They dump all kinds of stuff in it, and it's probably the raccoon's primary source of drinking water."

"Then how come we haven't seen more types of roadkill, like deer and skunk?" asked Frosby.

"Could be the chemicals in the river are only lethal to raccoons," offered Wilmart.

"Yeah, like that sounds plausible," replied Frosby snidely.

"Well, what's your theory, Mr. Councilman, sir?"

"My theory is that it's just a fluke of nature."

"Thank you for that. Explains a lot," mumbled Wilmart, letting out a loud sigh.

"Where they taking all the bodies?" inquired Lyle Sumner, manager of the Mini-Soda variety store.

"They're going to burn the carcasses out at the landfill, Lyle," replied Frosby.

"Did they test them first to determine how they died?" asked Wilmart, in a challenging tone.

"Macy, for heaven's sake, they died from being run over. We're not going to do autopsies on flattened roadkill. Cripes!"

"Then we're never going to know why a hundred animals died at the same time."

"Not quite at the same time. Over a forty-eight hour period," corrected Frosby.

"Oh, sure. That's not unusual at all," grumbled Wilmart.

"Okay, folks, meeting adjourned. The matter is being taken care of. If anything further develops, I'll let you know."

*   *   *

By noon the next day, another seventy raccoons had been found dead on the streets and roads of Hillsboro. Locals were beginning to panic, convinced that something dangerous confronted their small community. At another impromptu meeting on the issue, Herb Ramsey once again argued his hypothesis that raccoons were committing group termination. His words were met with hostility from Councilman Frosby.

"Will you just keep your dumb idea to yourself, Herb? It doesn't help matters."

"What's so dumb about it?" piped in Lyle. "Don't hear you coming up with anything better. Maybe Herb has something there."

"There's a professor over at Gilliam College that can communicate with animals. Maybe he can find out what's happening here," suggested Wilmart.

"You mean Dr. Doolittle? He's a wacko. Jeez, Macy!"

"It's Dr. Cushing, and he's highly respected in some circles."

"Circle of Jerks, you mean," commented Mel Holland, of Holland Hardware.

Several men at the gathering chuckled, further incensing Wilmart.

"I think there's an upside to all this," offered Lyle.

"And what is that?" inquired Frosby, warily.

"We got almost two hundred raccoon bodies, right? How about we skin them and make some coats to sell?"

Silence descended over the assemblage, and then Herb spoke up.

"That ain't an entirely bad notion. Let 'em keep killing themselves, and we'll soon have a thriving business."

"That's such a disgusting and inhumane idea," spouted Wilmart, who was joined by a round of applause and then a chorus of loud chants.

"SAVE THE RACCOONS ... SAVE THE RACCOONS! "

"Okay ... okay, quiet down! Quiet! You're all out of order!" blurted Frosby.

Once the assemblage regained its composure, the discussion over the roadkill crisis continued. In the end, Frosby reluctantly agreed to enlist the aid of Professor Cushing.

"We got to catch a raccoon as it's about to leap in front of a car. Why don't we leave that to you, Herb? You seem to be on the scene all the time."

"No problem. I'll trap one and bring it to you, Ryan."

In a couple of hours, Herb was back at the town offices with a cat carrier containing a raccoon that had failed in its attempt to kill itself.

"Good job, Herb. Turn him over to Macy. She'll take it to Dr. Doo … ah, what's his name. He's agreed to check it out."

Two hours later, Professor Cushing was addressing the raccoon as it looked out at him from inside its cage. Less than a day later Macy was contacted by Cushing, who informed her that the raccoon had communicated to him.

"Please come to Hillsboro, Dr. Cushing. We're all eager for your report."

At the appointed hour, the professor arrived at the town offices with the trapped raccoon.

"So, Professor, you claim that coon talked to you?" asked Frosby, nodding at the carrier.

A few snickers erupted up from the crowd.

"Shoosh," bellowed Wilmart. "Let the good doctor speak."

"So what'd the little bandit have to say about all its furry friends jumping in front of cars," asked Frosby, cynically.

"Well, the young *Procyon lotor*, as raccoons are formally called, said …"

The professor hesitated here, causing the members of the audience to lean forward in their folding chairs.

"Yes, professor? Go ahead. What did it say about all its dead brethren?" urged Frosby.

Clearing his throat, the professor continued. "It said … '*Life is meaningless.*'"

#

Big Black Car

*When the body and material substance of it
has altogether vanished like a dream.*
— Thomas Carlyle

Mavis looked into his rearview mirror and saw a big black car behind him. When he checked his driver's side mirror, the big black car was not there. Nor was the big black car evident when he checked his passenger's side mirror. He returned his gaze to the rearview mirror and found that the big black car was not only there but had moved closer. Again, he looked into his side view mirrors and was relieved to see the big black car, although it was only inches from his bumper. When he turned his attention back to the rearview mirror, the big black car was no longer there. It was at that moment that Mavis experienced intense pressure in his ears and felt weightless. To his total astonishment, the big black car was now in front of him. Then it was gone, and the road before him opened to the stars.

#

AUTHOR'S BIO

Michael C. Keith is the author of more than 20 books on electronic media, among them *Talking Radio, Voices in the Purple Haze, Radio Cultures, Signals in the Air*, and the classic text book *The Radio Station*. The recipient of numerous awards in his academic field, he is also the author of dozens of journal articles and short stories and has served in a variety of editorial positions. In addition, he is the author of an acclaimed memoir—The Next Better Place (screenplay co-written with Cetywa Powell), a young adult novel—*Life is Falling Sideways*, and five other story anthologies—*Of Night and Light, Everything is Epic, And Through the Trembling Air, Sad Boy*, and *Hoag's Object*. He has been nominated for two Pushcart Prizes and a Pen/O.Henry Award and was a finalist for the National Indie Excellence Award for short Fiction Anthology and a finalist for the 2013 International Book Award in the 'Fiction Visionary' category.

www.ingramcontent.com/pod-product-compliance
Lightning Source LLC
Chambersburg PA
CBHW022124170626
46808CB00002B/828